Mr. Finney

A HERO IN TIME

Best of luck !

P

A HERO IN TIME

Peter J. Rappa, M.D.

One Book *at a* **Time**
Addison, Texas

A HERO IN TIME

© 2016 Peter J. Rappa, M.D.

Cover designed by Monica Rappa

Photo taken by Cityography

Special Assistance with Production by Ann Vyers

Manufactured in the United States of America.

For information, please go to:

www.peterrappa.com

ISBN: 978-0-9895333-9-3

With Thanks to the Special Souls
who fill my life with Joy

To Providence, Betty Rappa
My Mother
Thank you for being the source of selfless love

To Rosana Rappa Butler
Sister, Editor
Thank you for being the
Sounding Board in Soul Work

To Monica
Wife, Life Partner, Soul Mate
Thank you for your Love and Support

To Tessa Ariel Rappa
Soul Time 18:15
Thank you for your Toughness

To Paloma Alexandria Rappa
Soul Time 18:18
Thank you for your Kindness

To Marina Rose Rappa
Soul Time 18:20
Thank you for your Tender Heartedness

Make me a channel of your peace.

Where there is hatred let me bring your love.

Where there is injury, your pardon,

And where there is doubt true faith.

O master grant that I may never seek

So much to be consoled as to console,

To be understood, as to understand,

To be loved as to love with all my soul.

For it is in giving that we receive,

In pardoning that we are pardoned,

And in dying that we are born to eternal life.

The Prayer of St. Francis

CHAPTER 1

Sunday, July 1, 2012

Steward Township Hospital
Meza, Texas
Residents Call Room

01:30 AM

The obnoxious staccato of beeps penetrated Dr. Jason Williams' awareness. Dr. Williams did not even have to turn on the wall light in the darkened call room to check the pager, as he knew that sound by heart. Level I trauma: rooftop. Awake, he pulled himself upright in the top bunk bed in the dorm style call room, yawned, and checked the clock. One thirty AM. No surprise, he shrugged, the bars are just about to close, the gang bangers are still cruising, and the night crawlers are out in force. Over the last four years as a general surgery resident it seemed the middle of the night was the best time for assaults, injury and collisions.

Already in green scrubs, Dr. Williams grabbed his phone, keys and cinched the ICU pager to his drawstring as well as the trauma pager. He slipped on his surgical clogs and headed out of the narrow tunnel-like basement closet that served as his bedroom nearly every third night over the last four years.

Dr. Williams arrived to the rooftop, where he met Dr. Aaron Jones, the senior Emergency Medicine Resident, and one of the ER nurses, Shelly B. In scrubs, sans lab coats, the three of them waited together on the rooftop helipad where a big orange 'X' marked the landing spot of the newest arrival.

"Who are we expecting?" Williams asked Jonesy.

"Oh, you know," Jonesy replied, "just another someone, that was somewhere they shouldn't have been, doing something they shouldn't have been doing."

"Somebody, somewhere, doing something they shouldn't have been doing ... sounds like a country and western song," Shelly B shot back and began to whistle the melody of 'Somebody Done Somebody Wrong Song.' "BJ Thomas, American Song writer, released circa 1975," she said as she walked toward the intercom for intel on the incoming victim.

"An error in judgment, huh," Williams played along, but as soon as he said it, he checked over his shoulder hoping there was no one behind him to hear it.

"There's no one behind you, Dr. Chief Resident," Jonesy said to Williams, taking note of Dr. Williams' flinch. "Dr. Mac would have a problem with that," Williams said, "especially coming from his new chief resident."

"Yeah, Dr. Mac sure has a unique way of looking at things," Jonesy said referring to Dr. Jon Mackenzie, the steward of the residency program and chairman of the department of surgery. "But look he's changed you ... you've been Chief Resident now for what – two hours? And he has already got you looking over your shoulder ... like all proper and stuff. And where is your intern dude? Shouldn't you have an intern tailing you?"

"You know where my intern is Jonesy," Williams laughed along.

"Yeah, probably half way to Austin by now; and tell me Dr. Williams; why did you let your intern go early?" Jonesy went on.

Dr. Williams just smiled and played along, and as if on cue replied, " 'because every kindness counts!' " Jonesy and Williams burst out in laughter as soon as the Dr. Mackenzie-ism was released from Dr. Williams' lips. "I bet Dr. Mac will say that a hundred times before Christmas," Jonesy quipped.

"Incoming," Dr. Jones said as he heard the air being beat back in a rotational thudder, thudder, thudder.

"It's supposed to be a motorcycle accident, respiratory compromise, tubed in the field," Shelley B, said returning to the two, as she surfed the stretcher into the ready position.

"Same story, different day," Dr. Jones added looking up listening to the thudder, watching the bright colored helo wobbling in an inebriated spiral as it hovered without descending.

"Is it stuck or what?" Dr. Jones asked, hands on his hips, looking up at the sky.

"I don't think they plan on landing," Williams said as a rescue basket attached to a cable appeared over his head dropping down from the sky.

"What! What's all this!" Dr. Jones remarked laughing in disbelief, as the rescue basket approached lower now, taking form.

"Are you bleepin' kidding me?" Dr. Jones exclaimed as he stepped back as the basket hit the deck.

In the rescue basket rhythmically depressing an ambu bag attached to a field placed ET tube sat a paramedic dressed more like a combat soldier than an EMT.

"Here, breathe him," the paratrooper paramedic exclaimed hurriedly handing over the ambu bag – a football shaped oval plastic device that produced a bellows effect with each compression providing oxygen to the injured victim with each squeeze. "I've got to go back up … we can't land. No sled."

"Can't land? What are you talking about?" Jonesy

said in disbelief, unloading the victim. "Can't land, no sled," came the response from the paramilitary paramedic pointing up to the wobbling helo that under further inspection was missing the landing frame.

"You can't just drop him and then fly away!" Jonesy shouted up to the paramedic.

But it was already too late. As soon as Shelly B secured the transfer from the basket to the gurney, the basket was lifting back into the air, and the paratrooper paramedic was back up in the helo, and the helicopter was gone as quickly as it arrived.

"What is he wearing?" Jonesy exclaimed in disbelief, assessing the casualty.

"A parachute!" Shelly B replied.

"A parachute! Really?"

"Yes really; P A R A C H U T E – parachute; a device used to slow the motion of an object through an atmosphere by creating drag, or by providing aerodynamic lift." Shelly B explained.

"Jesus H. Christ," Dr. Jones said to Dr. Williams. "This guy must have really ticked them off. They were ready to throw him out of the chopper."

The body on the stretcher seemed to sense his new surroundings and woke up in a fit. He abraded the skin on his already burned and bruised face as he thrashed, and the eyes that were mere slits began profusely tearing. He began padding the air around him as if searching for something missing.

"Hey Shelly B – push some Ativan?" Dr. Williams instructed.

"He must think he is flying!" Jonesy added. "Can you say delirium!"

"Delirium; D E L E R I U M – delirium: An acute confusional state with attention processing deficits and severe perceptual disturbances sometimes with psychotic features like hallucinations and delusions. Often triggered by narcotics and benzodiazepines."

"Like the Ativan you just ordered," Jonesy added sarcastically.

"Give him the Ativan. We don't want him really flying. We'll deal with the acute confusional state on the back end."

"Vitamin A in!"

"Man ... a parachute ... not even landing.... This is a first for me," Williams said ruminating on the occurrence.

"Well this is a last for me," Jonesy said, looking at his watch marking time. "I am out after this shift."

"Graduation day huh Jonesy!" Williams responded, acknowledging June 30, the last day of the medical year.

"Yep! A new year will have started by the time I finish the paperwork on this fish," Dr. Jones said referring to the casualty in the basket who was thrashing about like a fish caught in a net.

"But carry on my wayward son. One more year for you right!"

"One more year," Williams said passing the gurney ahead to Shelly B. "One more year, then freedom," Jonesy said depressing the ambu bag in rhythm, as the three rolled the twenty-something year old un-named patient into the ER.

"One more year, then it's hearts for me," Dr. Williams allowed himself to indulge in a moment of projection, anticipating a fellowship in Cardiothoracic surgery next year in Houston: a fellowship that did not include rooftop airdrops in a wobbly basket from a chopper with no sled and no information.

"See if the fly boys stuffed any info into the package," Jonesy said. "Maybe he's carrying some type of ID."

Underneath the parachute the trauma victim was wearing a tee shirt and cargo pants. Williams unzipped the leg pockets on the cargo pant legs.

"Just a picture with a note attached," Williams said out loud looking at a heart shaped earring that secured the note to the back of the Polaroid photo.

"Looks old," Williams said, holding the Polaroid feeling the tattered fray of the clear protective scotch-tape.

"Note says, 'The Dive Shop, July 4th … be there!'"

"Not going to 'be there,'" Jonesy said as he passed the items to Shelly B. "July 4th," Shelly said; "we celebrate American Independence Day on the Fourth of July every year. We think of July 4, 1776, as a day that represents the Declaration of Independence and the birth of the United States of America as an independent nation." Shelly held the note and flipped it over and back once.

"Hmmnn, that's strange," Shelly said looking at the note.

"What's strange," Jonesy asked.

"It's from here," Shelly said.

"What do you mean it's from here?" Williams asked.

"The note. It's from here," and Shelly B re-pinned the note to the Polaroid picture through the top center header, a header that read 'Steward Township Hospital'.

"Ah ha … a mystery," Jonesy quipped.

"Mystery," Shelly B chimed in, as if at a grade school spelling bee; "a religious belief based on divine revelation, especially one regarded as beyond human understanding."

"Well it's definitely beyond my understanding," Jonesy said to Shelly the spelling bee queen. "We'll all ponder that as we resuscitate the crack head in the basket," Jonesy quipped quickening the pace of the stretcher into the ER doors.

Shelly B zippered the pant pocket closed, and began surfing the stretcher forward.

"Why don't you page your intern and get admit orders started on this lost boy, while I get him on a machine," Jonesy said referring to a ventilator. "We can roll him to CT as soon as his numbers look good and he is stable on the vent," Jonesy said to Williams, both of them knowing that the victim required brain imaging immediately.

"Sounds good," Williams called back, reflexively, before realizing there was no intern to rely on. Last day of the medical year technically ended at midnight last night even though most of the on-call residents would not be released from their responsibilities until 0600 this morning. So the new intern, even if he showed up on Sunday, would be brand new, and even if he was here, there would be no way he would be able to get orders started without a lot of hand holding.

'Last day First day,' Williams thought to himself pondering the arbitrary nature of time itself. 'Jonesy may be out after this one, but I am still in. All in the game baby,' Williams thought to himself. 'All in....'

———

The Emergency Room medical team received the new arrival taking immediate action. The unnamed patient was placed on a ventilator, same tube re-taped, and dressings were applied to the facial abrasions and blisters; in the space of ten minutes the patient was rolling to CT.

"Sorry, they can't scan him," Jonesy said as he and Shelley B parked the patient in Radiology.

"Why not?" Williams asked.

"Not in the computer. They need orders. Didn't your intern write him up yet? Oh that's right, he's not here, is he. You don't think he phoned them in from Austin, do you?"

"OK ... OK, watch him for me; let me see what I can do."

Usually by now, William's intern would have searched out the details, such as name, age and demographic info, and written out admit orders. Usually by now, Miss Treese, the night shift unit clerk who was both registrar and commander of the gate, would have him in the computer. But in this case, there were no details, and there was no intern to write orders. Williams walked over to the desk hoping for a bit of good luck.

"Hey Miss Treese," Williams asked the night shift clerk at the admitting station in the ER. "I was hoping you can help me out with a bit of a problem."

Miss Treese, wearing a traditional white one-piece nurses dress, just raised her dark brown eyes above her reading glasses and smiled a sarcastic smile.

"Well, don't ya know, Dr. Williams. Nice of you to join us," replied Miss Treese. "I've been paging your intern for twenty minutes, now."

"Oh … well he's, he's not here…."

"I can see that don't ya know. And I need orders on your new admission, Dr. Williams; you see a new patient arrived in a wobbling helicopter, don't ya know, supposedly missing a landing sled. Don't ya know, the young men were wearing parachutes and threw him out of the plane."

"They were wearing parachutes, Miss Treese. But they did not throw him out of the plane."

"Oh, so you know about that one there, then?"

"Yes, I was there Miss Treese. Jonesy and I just caught that trauma – lowered him down in a rescue basket. Didn't Jonesy and Shelly B just wheel by here?"

"Oh yes they did Dr. Williams … said your intern had the details … but, don't ya know, no intern responding, going on twenty minutes now Dr. Williams don't ya know."

"Oh about that, Miss Treese, I'm afraid I let my intern go early."

"Well how about that doctor. So you gonna write admission orders, doctor?"

"Yes, Miss Treese. I'll write him up. But first I can use a little help. Can you get him in the system Stat.

Radiology won't Cat Scan him unless he has a medical record number. Can you get him in?"

"Well now, don't ya know. Last name and last four of his social?"

"Ummm; not sure. After all he did just drop out of a chopper in a rescue basket."

"OK drivers license number."

"Ummmm not really sure. He didn't have any ID. And I don't think the paratroopers stopped in to register him, did they?"

Miss Treese just peered up at Dr. Williams over the top of her glasses with a 'are you kidding me' look.

"Well then I don't suppose you got his insurance card?"

"No Miss Treese, I'm afraid not."

"So what you are telling me is that you don't know anything, don't ya know."

"That's right, Miss Treese. I know nothing. But I do know he needs to get imaged. And radiology cannot scan him without a medical record number. Can you assign him a number and get him in the computer so I can get him imaged?"

"OK, let's assign *the unassigned* a number. That one there, with no identity, no details…. And *Doctor Williams*, no insurance card, don't ya know?"

Ms. Treese looked at her watch and began to type.

"He is TV One Forty Four Oh Six ... Doctor," Miss Treese exclaimed, pressing enter on her computer as she lifted her eyes up from her wrist watch.

"Trauma Victim One Forty Four, Oh Six," Williams acknowledged as if synchronizing his watch with hers. "Got it. Trauma Victim 14406."

"Thank you Miss Treese. I'm writing out orders right now; and after I get him into the scanner, I will call the attending."

"Oh, no need, don't ya know. He already knows. I called him for ya Dr. Williams. See, I couldn't get a hold of the intern don't ya know. Specific instructions now Doctor. Someone don't respond, we call the attending on call. Dr. Childs is waiting for your call."

"OK, thanks Ms. Treese, you are a lifesaver" Williams said sarcastically.

"Now that's true, don't ya know," she said smiling.

Dr. Williams picked up the phone ready to face the music. He paused mid stance when Jonesy walked by with a clipboard in his hand. "Hey doctor 'every-kindness-counts'; I've got a better one for ya."

"Oh yeah, what's that Jonesy," Williams went along.

"How about 'no good deed goes unpunished.' Still think it was a good idea to let your intern go early?"

"He has to be in Austin tomorrow and I didn't want him to drive post call. I thought it was for the greater good. Every kindness counts, you know," Williams quipped to Jonesy.

"Oh, don't you even go there," Jonesy said rolling his eyes at the Dr. Mac-ism.

"I don't suppose you want to call this one in to Dr. Childs, do you?" Williams asked Jonesy.

"Wild Bill Childs? Is he on tonight … no, I don't want to call it in, but I want to hear you tell him."

———

Sunday July 1, 2012
Steward Emergency Room
Physician workstation
02:00 AM

"Williams?"

"Hi Dr. Childs, yes its me."

"Why is there no Intern, Jason?"

"I let him go sir … he's supposed to be in Austin tomorrow; it is June 30th, after all … really July 1st already."

"Well why wasn't I informed, Jason."

"Sorry sir, I didn't think it was that much of a problem. I've got it covered sir."

"Well what's this I hear about this new trauma? I hear the air evac group is unregistered and they just dumped a level one injury on our rooftop. If they don't explain this they will never fly again. I'll have their license for this!"

"Yes, sir," Williams said as Jonesy chuckled out of earshot. "I understand, sir. Jonesy and I just got the page and we caught it."

"Tell him he sort of just landed in our lap," Jonesy cackled from the background. "We wanted to send him back but the bird was like Blackhawk Down!"

"Nobody cleared any of this with me tonight, Jason … what kind of outfit just falls in from the sky without calling ahead."

"Yes, sir…. I mean I don't know sir," Williams looked over to Jonesy with his hands up.

"Well what on earth happened?" Dr. Childs asked.

"Tell him … tell him …" Jonesy paused briefly collecting his thoughts, like Cyrano de Bergerac feeding lines to Christian. "Tell him the synchronistic forces of the universe came together to create a vortex in the continuum of time and he was lowered down through a wormhole in a wobbling helicopter with no sled. Tell him that."

Williams rolled his eyes at Jonesy and went on.

"He arrived in a rescue basket suspended by a cable, sir. The patient hit the roof wearing civilian clothes, no ID. He had a parachute strapped on his back. The rescue team was still pumping his ambu bag when they dropped him down on the cable. They took off in hurry sir, their helicopter was a wobbling mess, sir; they didn't stay long enough to give us any details sir," Williams finally finished.

"OK Jason, we'll see about all of this tomorrow. But I'll tell you this; there will be hell to pay for this."

"Yes, sir."

"Well how is the trauma? Is he stable?"

"Yes, sir," Dr. Williams went on. "He came in with a tube already down him; we re-taped him; he is doing well on the vent, and we are getting him imaged right now."

"Where's he going to Jason?"

"He's in CT now, should be there for the next twenty minutes, then he's going to ICU bed-1."

"OK what's his name?"

"No name sir, we're working on getting ID," Williams cringed as he looked at Jonesy who was just beside himself.

"God damn it Williams, I know this is your first day as chief resident, but … first you let the intern go, and now this. A no information drop-in without prior authorization or Attending consent!"

"Sorry sir…."

"OK, give me his MR number so I can find him in the computer."

Williams looked at his watch recalling the time he and Miss Treese logged the no information patient in at.

"One-forty-four-oh-six, Sir."

"One forty four oh six," Dr. Childs repeated, "got it."

"OK I am on my way."

CHAPTER 2

July 1, 2012

Steward Township Hospital
Radiology Suite

02:15 AM

In a state between awake and asleep Trauma Victim One-forty-four-oh-six or TV 14406 as he was now called, awakened. He tried to open his eyes, but they weighed as much as bricks, and they were too heavy for him to overcome. He tried to speak, but immediately began choking and bit down against something hard, like the tailpipe of his dirt bike. TV 14406 tried to move, but the more he struggled, the weaker he became. Blinded and paralyzed, he felt mummified, as sound from the outside world echoed in his mind.

"One-forty-four-oh-six. CT brain," TV 14406 heard from within his uncommunicative state within the darkness, as his body lie motionless on a moving table.

"One forty four oh six," ruminated Trauma Victim 14406 within his delirium. "The Thorpedo!" He shouted silently in a burst of realization, the endotracheal tube smothering words into inaudible sounds. "One minute, forty four seconds and six one-hundredths of a second Mr. S! Can you believe it?" asked TV 14406 to the ether.

"He's moving!" Dr. Childs shouted into the speaker from outside the viewing room of the CT scanner.

The tech watched TV 14406 clutch at air, arms restrained by white cloth ties, hands secured in big white boxing-glove-like mittens. Unable to move his arms against the restraints that held him in check, TV 14406 tried to swing his legs as if to move himself off the bed, before he finally fatigued.

"Back him out!" said Dr. Childs from the control room viewing area to the radiology tech operating the table. The tech pressed a button and spoke into the microphone.

"Backing out," the operator said, pressing a button to bring the table back in from the CT scanner tunnel. The radiology tech operating the CT scanner paused the moving table outside the tunnel and checked on the status of his patient...

"Push some more Versed!"

"The record, Mr. Sebastian," TV 14406 silently called to his old coach. "1:44.06 is the world record for two hundred meters freestyle. The record, Mr. Sebastian; remember? Each fifty faster than the last! Freestyle, Mr. S!" And the body of TV 14406 tried to flap his arms like a big bird prior to take off.

"Christ Jesus, he's still moving!" came the voice from within the speaker, watching TV 14406 pushing up hard against the restraints.

"We studied that swim, Mr. Sebastian." Andrew said to his old coach from within clouded consciousness. "We studied it before I left for California," he said in thought as his focus left the present and drifted into the depths of his mind. ... I was the best I had ever been, Mr. Sebastian ... training with you. California was a bust for me, Mr. Sebastian."

"Give him some Vitamin A," Dr. Childs said to the tech operator referring to Ativan. "Make sure he doesn't break free," Dr. Childs said to the tech operator.

"Already gave him one half of the Versed, Doc," the tech replied.

"Well it didn't touch him," came the response from the console. "Just go ahead and push the rest of the Versed," instructed the doctor.

The tech walked over to the table, picked up the syringe loaded with the sedative and injected it into the rubber IV tubing watching the saline fluid carry the sedative into the patient's vein.

"Versed in ... he should be quiet in a minute or two."

"Check him out; make sure he is OK before you send him back in. I don't want this guy to extubate himself in the CT scanner," Dr. Childs said, speaking into the microphone, referring to losing the endotracheal tube that was situated in TV 14406's pharynx attached to the ventilator that was breathing for him.

The tech inspected his patient. The moistened 2x2 gauze covering the eyes of the victim were intact. The Endotracheal tube that emerged from the victim's cracked lips ran to a connector attached to blue tubing, and like a dual exhaust the dual tubing made its way to a ventilator outside the CT scanner.

"Eyes covered, tube looks OK!"

"Dim all the lights" Dr. Childs' voice appeared again from the console speaker.

"Why do you want to dim the lights?" asked the tech.

"PCP is a hallucinogen – makes lights flash, and they see halos ... makes them want to move."

"Oh ... I get it ... fight the light, fight the light," laughed the tech. "Or move toward it ... you never know right?"

"Is he positive for PCP?" Dr. Williams asked Dr. Childs as they waited for the imaging to be completed.

"Probably, by the sounds of things Jason; probably high as a kite. He was wearing a parachute when he hit the ER, right?"

"Yes sir."

"Probably wanted to fly. But either way the last thing we want is for him to wake up and try to sit up in the scanner …"

The radiology tech watched the restless patient fight against the restraints. From the table TV 14406 mustered all the power he could summon. Suddenly, Trauma Victim 14406 pulled up against the restraints in a full body effort as if he was launching himself from the starting block at the beginning of a race.

"Did you push the Versed yet?" came the voice from the screen, as Dr. Childs waited outside the CT scanner.

"It went in like seven minutes ago," the tech replied, looking at his watch, jumping back as the body unexpectedly heaved up like a volcano.

"Who is this guy, superman?"

"No, Superman doesn't need a parachute to fly."

"Very funny – give him another amp and knock him the heck out," Dr. Childs ordered. "The last thing we need is head injury on top of a brain injury," Dr. Childs added.

"OK, Dr. Childs. You got it."

"Sweet dreams Superman," the tech said sending more sedative in through the IV.

As the warmth produced by the anesthetic coursed its way into his system, TV 14406 stopped fighting.

"OK," Dr. Childs gave the order to the tech. "Go, Go, Go!"

With his body etherized on the table, the consciousness of TV 14406 was set free.

As the body of TV 14406 progressed forward back into the CT scan tunnel, the untethered awareness of TV 14406 responded to the call. "Go, Go, Go!" he heard.

"Training day he said to himself. I've got to get up. Training day."

CHAPTER 3

August 1, 2004

California Swim Club

"Go, Goo, Goo!" Andrew Galloway heard each time he rotated his head up and out of the water to take a breath.

"Go, Goo, Goo!" He heard as the coach pounded out the beat with each stroke Andrew swam. From within the water in lane one of the eight lane Olympic sized pool, Andrew watched the short, stout coach walk alongside him, pounding a clipboard against his thigh, exhorting Andrew to pull faster as he glided in freestyle through the water.

Andrew briefly picked up his turnover and rotated his hips and arms faster with each freestyle pull. He quickened the rate of flutter kicks and his legs added power like a propeller powering a submarine. Andrew went faster over the next eight or ten strokes and immediately geared down as he felt a knot threatening to cramp his left thigh. He glided through the water in cruising speed, barely kicking and in three strokes he touched the wall, picked his head up, and took a deep breath looking right up at the banner that read "Welcome to The California Swim Club, home of the 2004 Championships."

"Hey Galloway," Andrew heard from the coach above the pool holding the clipboard. "You have to sprint to win! Not coast!" the booming voice echoed throughout the natatorium before going on. "The purpose of time trials is to make time. You know that right!"

Andrew just nodded his head. Andrew made his way to the ladder, and climbed up the steps of the ladder instead of hoisting himself up over the edge of the pool in the usual way, trying to protect his thigh from cramping and avoid putting added stress on his left knee.

"The ladder Galloway? Really?" Mr. Mendonhall watched in amazement.

Andrew kept his head down, avoiding eye contact with the coach and grabbed his towel and began to walk off when Mr. Mendonhall caught up to him.

"What's wrong Galloway. You are swimming like an old lady out there."

"Sorry Mr. Mendonhall."

"That time up there," Mr. Mendonhall pointed to the scoreboard, "is not even close to what you need."

"I know Mr. Mendonhall."

"You know you have managed to go slower; each week since you have been here, your times have gotten slower," Mr. Mendonhall said.

"Yes, I know, Mr. Mendonhall."

"What happened Galloway? What happened to the East Coast Ace who first arrived at my doorstep?"

"I'm sorry Mr. Mendonhall. I'm not sure what changed," Andrew said to his coach knowing exactly what had changed.

Andrew had been invited to the California Swim Club because he had success as a junior. It was a great opportunity to train with the best. It was a real opportunity to step up his fitness training in a state of the art complex, work on stroke production by underwater camera analysis, and train with other athletes who had their sites set on Nationals. He, like everyone else, thought this was real opportunity: opportunity to win and go on in the sport. At the time, moving up seemed exciting: Nationals, maybe even with enough time and enough training, Olympics. What kid wouldn't want that?

At the California Swim club, Andrew was up at six, water workouts were followed by analysis and stroke production, which was followed by weights, with food stuffed in during free time and breaks to keep up with the enormous caloric expenditure. The physical training was tough, but he expected it; even enjoyed it. What he didn't expect, and what he didn't enjoy was the undercurrent of pressure. Under Mr. Mendonhall's tutelage winning was at the core. Lift the most; sprint the fastest; first in; always first, always strive to win. While Andrew knew results were important, it was a distinct departure from Mr. Sebastian's philosophy and training style.

Shortly after his arrival in California, Andrew felt things change. For Andrew, the thrill was gone. As the days and weeks passed, the sarcasm and pressure took its toll on him. Andrew wasn't sure exactly when, but swimming and training became work instead of a labor of love that he had known under Mr. Sebastian. Dispirited, injury followed, and he couldn't shake a sore left knee and a thigh that kept cramping. It was if his legs had been taken right out from underneath him.

As his knee hurt and his thigh cramped, his times slowed down and he found it harder and harder to compete. Soon he went from swimming lead in workouts to following, and now he was last in the lane – last where the slowest swimmer swims.

"I don't understand it Galloway. You did so well in juniors. You came here with so much potential. What happened?"

"I don't know Mr. Mendonhall. When I first began swimming with Mr. Sebastian there was real joy in it, you know?"

"Joy? Probably because you were consistently winning."

"But that's just it, Mr. Mendonhall. Mr. Sebastian and I didn't really talk about winning ... or losing."

"I don't see how anyone can call themselves a coach without talking about winning or losing. Sounds like a kook to me."

"He is not a kook, Mr. Mendonhall. I am beginning to think he was right. Right about everything."

"Like what?"

"Mr. Sebastian said that why you swim is as important as that you swim."

"In it to win it Galloway. That is how the big boys play."

"Mr. Sebastian would disagree. Mr. Sebastian had us focus on effort. He said effort was its own reward."

"Effort is it's own reward? I don't know if I agree with that Galloway. Winning is the reward."

"Winning a race is a byproduct of what you have become. A byproduct of the speed you have by being what you have become. Mr. Sebastian cautioned about focusing on anything but effort, commitment to principal and dedication to training."

"Cautioned you? About winning?"

"He said to beware of loss and gain; fame and shame. He said they were the opposite sides of the same coin, and both were low power states."

"So what did he have you focus on?"

"With Mr. Sebastian, I was committed ... to the art of the swim. 'Master the art of the swim,' he would say, 'and you will discover your perfect self.'"

"You don't have to be perfect in the water, Galloway. You just have to get to the other side first. Be fast; be first; that's what you need to focus on. Just win."

"I am not even sure I know how to do that anymore."

Andrew knew his passion for swimming and training had eroded to the point of extinction. It was a tough lesson, but Andrew realized Mr. Sebastian was right. All this time it was Andrew's love of doing that powered him forward.

"With Mr. Sebastian I was dropping time, swimming better and better, faster and faster."

"And you were winning."

"Yes, I was winning ... but I can see now that I was winning because I had become fast; not necessarily because I was trying to win."

"Not trying to win? That makes sense watching you compete now."

Andrew became quiet again feeling the truth of his soul. He knew this was not the time to try to explain how training and effort could be fulfilling in its own right; how being lost in the effort was joyful.

"And just how did your old coach have you master the art of the swim?"

"Attention to form was the first thing. He wouldn't tolerate sloppy stroke mechanics."

"That's why we have underwater cameras and spend time each day in video analysis."

"Then body ... we trained on land and in the water."

"That is why we have a world class training center here."

"Then there is mind and mindset; that is where there is real power, he believed."

"The mind of winner ... I agree. At some point, you've got to be able to look down those lanes at the other swimmers lining up next to you, and tell yourself you can beat them. That you can win. That is the mindset you've got to strive for."

"No ... I don't want to beat anyone, Mr. Mendonhall. When that time comes I want to be in the state of no-mind."

"No mind? Sometimes I think you are out of your mind Galloway."

"Yes ... out of mind is no mind. It is the quiet calm; the state of confidence without doubt. Getting to that state is the hallmark of mastery. Right now, all I am is doubt. And right now, I'm not sure I can win a club summer swim meet, let alone win against any of these guys," Andrew said pointing to the lead swimmers in each lane of the eight lane pool.

"He didn't want you to come here, did he?"

"Mr. Sebastian? No, he's not that way. He would never stand in my way. He's just not like that."

"So let me ask you; why did you come here Galloway?"

"It sounded exciting ... and after I got the invite...."

"Let me tell you why you came here Galloway: to become a champion Galloway. That is why you came here. Just like these other kids."

Andrew looked around at the other swimmers, getting ready for their next set. Coach Mendonhall was right. The promise of winning and going on was alluring. Andrew thought he wanted that for himself. But now, he wasn't so sure.

"Look Galloway," coach Mendonhall said putting his hand on Andrew's shoulder. "Why don't you take some time off, rest up, and come back when you are ready to compete."

Andrew was relieved.... He knew he couldn't compete. At this point the thought of competing made him sick. Although he didn't admit it out loud, his mind knew the truth of his feelings. His feelings were telling him that maybe this was a mistake. Maybe he did not have what it takes.

When Mr. Mendonhall suggested time off, Andrew was glad to be let off the hook. He knew his heart wasn't in it here at the California Swim Club. If there was one thing he had learned training with Mr. Sebastian, it was heart first, then head ... and no mind.

But leaving the most prestigious program in the country? That was going to be a tough sell. The phone call that followed wasn't as bad as it could have been....

"Dad ... it's not working out here. I want to come out there with you and mom. Small town Texas is fine, I'm sure it has lots of charm ... I don't mind finishing my senior year there. Whatever school mom is working for will be fine ... it is only one year ... or, I was thinking, I can just begin in the cadet-training program at the end of the summer. I'll be eighteen at the end of the summer, old enough you know. What's that? The Naval Academy? Yes, I know it's very prestigious and all.... Yes, I have everything I need to complete the application ... just about ready to start on it.... What's that? Swimming? No, that's fine ... the season here is over anyway ... no, you don't have to check into training programs there. I thought I might train with you for the rest of the summer ... like the old days, dad. I thought it might be fun to use the cadet training requirements to cross train ... you know, just in case STATESIDE needs a few pilots down the road. OK; see you Monday, thanks dad ... love you."

Chapter 4

Sunday July 1, 2012

Steward Township Hospital
Meza, Texas
ER physician work room

03:30 AM

Dr. Jason Williams admitted Trauma Victim 14406 to Dr. Jon MacKenzie's service. Williams would have to present the details of the new patient tomorrow despite the limited details. 'Think like Jonesy,' Williams said to himself as he rehearsed his lines.

"This is TV 14406, a twenty somethingish-year-old male, injured we think in a high-speed motorcycle accident. He was air vac'd in last night."

I better leave out the editorialized comment that Jonesy had added, "where he was doing something he should not have been doing...."

"Has had stable vitals, has been combative at times, intubated and sedated in a cervical collar. He came in with no written information, and the outfit that dropped him in couldn't provide any details."

'One more year,' Williams thought. 'One more year of middle of the night drop and ditch's, paratrooper paramedics, a Chief of Service who thinks that every kindness counts and a nun who is to be escorted in daily who believes that every medical event is linked to the destiny of the soul ... whatever that is.'

Williams shook his head as he started down the hallway and said sarcastically, "The destiny of the soul, Miss Treese ... do you know what that is?"

"I don't know much about destiny, Dr. Williams, don't ya know. But I do know one thing; I'm gonna pray for *your soul*, from the looks of things you're gonna need it don't ya know."

"Praise the Lord," Dr. Williams, said laughing.

"Amen to that don't ya know ..." she said.

———

Friday July 1, 2012

Steward Township Hospital
Outside ICU Bed One

04:00 AM

"What does the chart say?" Captain Spence asked Specialist Sully, each of them out of their flight gear, still un-showered, but in civilian clothes.

"CT brain – no bleeding: some swelling though," came Specialist Sully's response.

"Spinal cord OK?" Captain Spence asked.

"Looks like it."

"Pretty bad road rash to his face; and apparently still swollen."

"Hey, that looks like the same tube I placed up in the air!" Sully observed from outside the window.

"Sully, Cappy, put the chart down, someone is coming," Lt. Pete called out standing guard outside Andrew's room.

"OK, no details. Let me do the talking," Captain Spence instructed Specialist Sully, while giving Lieutenant Pete the signal to evacuate the hallway.

"Hello there doctors; are any of you taking care of him?"

"We are the Critical Care Specialists consulting on this case. But he is admitted to the Trauma team. Dr. Williams is on call tonight; he is the chief resident. Is something wrong."

"Oh, no, well how is he doing?"

"I'm sorry, and who are you?"

"Can't say really; but we were there last night when he came in on the rooftop."

"Oh, is that right? Do you know this young man? Because he is admitted as a no information patient and we would love to get a name and accurate demographics."

"Can't really say but, I did hear that the patient there had received more than one amp of sux prior to drop-in, and I just wanted the doc's here to know that, just in case that information would be helpful."

"Oh, yes, very helpful, yes," the physician in charge replied. "Succinylcholine, a paralytic. Multiple doses of paralytics combined with sedative hypnotics can produce quite a problem with respiratory suppression, not to mention quite a delirium."

"OK," the chief addressed his group of six doctors in staggered white coats. "Who can tell me about sux?"

"Succinylcholine, also known as suxamethonium is a nicotinic acetylcholine receptor agonist used to induce muscle relaxation or short term paralysis, typically for the purpose of tracheal intubation. It is sometimes used in combination with analgesics and sedatives for euthanasia, and immobilization of horses. In hospital parlance, it's colloquial known as 'SUX.'"

"Yes, very good. Now take a look at this patient. If he just received sux and versed, what would you expect to see on his exam?"

"No reflexes; and poor spontaneous breathing."

"Yes, very good. And as you can see, reflexes are returning, and he has begun breathing spontaneously."

"Yes, very good; very favorable prognosis for extubation."

"Yes, if we play it by the book, keep his numbers good, I foresee a spontaneous breathing trial shortly."

"Sorry Doctor, what does that mean?" Lieutenant Pete asked.

"It means that he should be breathing on his own very soon; without the tube or the machine."

"Oh, great! Then he should be waking up soon then?"

"I'm sorry, who did you say you are with?"

───────

Sunday, July 1, 2012
Steward Township Hospital
Intensive Care Unit Family Waiting Room
07:00 AM

Sister Mary Grace, of Grace of Souls Mission, sat in the first chair in a row of chairs in the waiting room outside the Intensive Care Unit. She sat quietly, perfectly still staring straight ahead into the body of the room enjoying the morning quiet.

At one minute past seven, Ginny Hawkins RN, red hair flowing loosely in navy blue scrubs and black clogs, walked up the corridor from the ICU to the waiting room where she found her package. Ginny took a moment to study the nun before completing her assignment to walk her in to the ICU. The nun was dressed in her familiar black habit with black head wrap accented by a white headband that emitted a glow as if absorbing the fluorescent lights above. Amazing, Ginny thought, then laughed. Amazing Grace!

"Good morning, Sister Mary Grace. Ready to sit with me?" Ginny broke the silence of the waiting room.

"Oh, good morning my child. Are you here to collect me?" Sister Mary Grace said while holding the young nurses' gaze for more than a moment.

"Yes, Sister, yes I am," Ginny responded with a smile as she felt the warmth offered by the nun's presence.

"We'll be working bed-1 today," Ginny said pausing a moment to study the circular arc of grey that travelled around the circumference of the Sister's irises; the arc of grey made a circle around the still vibrant blue center of her eyes and it gave the Sister a unique mystical glimmer Ginny thought.

"Exciting, isn't it?" Sister Mary Grace said to Ginny as the Sister smiled and stood up from the family room chair.

"What's that sister?" Ginny asked as she hooked the nun's arm.

"The excitement of the day. The promise of what can be," she said as she straightened the pleats of her long black robe.

"How do you do it, Sister?"

"Do what?"

"Feel such enthusiasm for something you have been doing for ... twenty years now Sister?"

"Oh, you are kind my dear ... twenty years ... she laughed. Sisters are we?" she said knowing she was old enough to be Ginny's grandmother.

"But seriously, how do you do it. You are always so happy, and your sense of humor sister, really. I wish I could have some of your high-energy enthusiasm."

"I am blessed my dear. I am blessed to be about the work of my soul. For me, there is a joy that comes from being here: from praying here, and from being around the many in distress who just need to be understood, and often times to be forgiven. Not to mention the joy I feel to be a part of the many wonderful doctors and nurses and techs that are so interesting and colorful. And young, I might add. So each day offers inner delight, my dear. In giving prayers and sending out love, I feel a sense of purpose, and at my age those days of living with purpose are surely becoming short. So let's make hay while the sun is shining, shall we?"

"You bet sister. Hay it is." Ginny said escorting the sister through the magnetic doors of the outer hall with a swipe of her name badge, into the ICU where she guided her to the bedside chair in room 1.

Ginny escorted Sister Mary Grace to the only chair in bed one of the ICU. With the back of her chair against the wall and below the hallway observation window that was attached to a workstation, the Sister sat out of sight of any hallway passersby, even those looking in from the open door. The room was small, not really intended for visitors. Despite its size, the room became a favorite for Sister Mary Grace who through the years had developed an amazing capacity to sit for hours at a time. Although she spent much of the time in silent prayer, 'keeping time' with the patients, she was known to often lift her voice in song, singing with perfect pitch. At other times, she could be seen to adopt a meditative pose with both feet firmly on the floor, spine straight and eyes locked on to a target that seemed to be telling her of its true essence. At times, of course, commensurate with her age, she would be known to nap as well – arms tucked together in the long sleeves of her robe, head down, eyes closed.

From outside the room, in the hallway, Ginny picked up the chart of her assignment. Ginny scanned the chart for any new orders while spot checking her monitors, frequently glancing up at her patient, and keeping one eye on the Sister. A moment later, Ginny walked back into the room and began assessing her patient.

"Who has come to see us today, my dear?" The Sister asked.

"That's funny Sister," Ginny said, the Sister's turn of a phrase evoking an appointment as if the patient had come to get his haircut.

"He did not have a name earlier, Sister, only a number," she said looking sideways at the patient in bed one. "Let's see what we can find."

Ginny made her way to the window side of the room passing up open packages of gauze, Neosporin, and Kerlex, and picked up a pair of cargo pants that were neatly folded over a tee shirt sitting on top of a folded parachute.

"A parachute! Really," she said and laughed.

Ginny went through the clothing and she smiled as she felt something in the pocket, and unzipped the pants. She found a Polaroid picture that was pierced by an earring in the shape of a heart; the earring was holding a note pinned to the back of the photo.

"Oh look; it's a picture and a note."

"What does the note say, my dear?" Sister Mary Grace asked.

"Dive Shop, July 4th … Be There!" Ginny read out loud, flipping the note over and back.

"The photo looks old, Sister, but the note looks new," she said scrunching her forehead reading the note's letterhead. "Steward Township Hospital?" Ginny looked up at the nun with a puzzled look.

"What about the photo?" Sister asked.

Ginny turned her attention to the old Polaroid feeling the texture of the weathered Polaroid protected by clear scotch tape looking past the figures in the photo. "He must have carried this with him every day," she said. Ginny glanced at the photo and then down to her patient trying to match a likeness with the two male participants in the action photo, but with little success. Looking down at her patient, she noticed the facial dressings were starting to dry and cake.

"No identification; Sister, only a note and an old Polaroid," She said taking note of the dressings.

"At some point today we'll need to change those dressings," she said out loud to the sister. "Don't want them too dry."

Ginny placed the Polaroid photo back in the cargos and zippered the pant pocket closed.

CHAPTER 5

"Polaroids," ruminated TV 14406 aroused into momentary awareness. In the blackness, he felt as if his eyes were sealed shut, the pressure of the pads too much to overcome, the paralytics sparing no muscle. The tube leaving his mouth muted Andrew's smile as his awareness was quickly set adrift as a bolt of pain riveted through his body.

August 26, 2004
Meza Texas

Andrew Galloway met the night sky as it gave way to morning light. He grabbed his phone; threw on some training shorts, stuffed a towel into his Backpack, grabbed a pair of goggles and slipped on blue jeans and a soft white cotton T-shirt with a V-neck that clung tightly to his broad shoulders and muscular back. He stepped lightly across the landing careful not to wake his mom, and slid down the stairs to the kitchen. At the refrigerator, he grabbed a bottle of water, an apple and closed the door. Andrew paused in front of the closed refrigerator door that was a maze of Polaroid photos taped to its surface. While marking his life in time, Andrew's eye was quickly drawn to a Polaroid picture of his father. His father was captured in a moment in time, with two fingers extended, stretched out toward the camera. With a smile, Andrew extended his fingers to match, just as in Michelangelo's portrait of God enlivening man. As Andrew's fingers made contact with the two fingers in the Polaroid, a sudden zap of static electricity surprised him and pushed him back one step.

"Shocking!" Andrew said, pondering the meaning of the unexpected occurrence.

"Huh: a glitch in the matrix," he smiled and found Mr. Sebastian's photo tacked down toward the bottom of the refrigerator door.

"A glitch in the matrix, right Mr. Sebastian …" Andrew said and laughed.

Andrew stopped to think about the moment he just experienced, wondering if such a thing was even possible. Was it possible that his father had been thinking about him at the exact moment that Andrew was thinking about his father? Was it possible that the co-incidence of thought transcended the matrix of time and space with an electric spark?

"What do you think, Mr. Sebastian, is that my dad reaching out to me?" Andrew asked the photo, pausing for a moment as if waiting for the refrigerator photo to reply back.

But Andrew knew the answer that would have followed. If he had asked Mr. Sebastian about chance, or co-incidence, Andrew knew exactly what his coach's comeback would be.

"There are no coincidences, Andrew, you must understand that. And there is no such thing as chance. Our perception is often just too limited. The unexpected events we call accidents are merely unanticipated outcomes."

Mr. Sebastian also believed that there was method to the madness.

"It is very simple, Andrew, really. We are all pulled forward by a force, attracted like a paperclip to a magnet, to a destiny that we know nothing of. In the matrix of time and space, with limited perception, we cannot always anticipate what comes our way. But what comes our way is opportunity. Opportunity to fulfill a destiny we often know little of: a destiny of the soul."

"Is there such a thing Mr. S? Is there a destiny of the soul?" Andrew said to the Polaroid before leaving the electric moment of reflection. "If so, I hope your soul work is complete," Andrew said finding the Polaroid of the silver haired coach with a stopwatch in his hand. "Dad ... see you when I see you; Mr. S ... time to go," Andrew said as he tapped the refrigerator door one last time. "Ha, ha that's funny ... 'time' to go," Andrew reflected feeling as if he had been fighting time, traveling through time all his life.

Andrew grabbed his gear and opened the back door; stepped up and down on the top steps a few time, supporting all his weight on the last step of the stair. His left knee no longer hurt and the swelling was gone; the knot in his right quad was fading, as was the memory of a training program of The California Swim Club; a memory and a program that he was happy to leave behind.

Andrew bent his knee then extended again, and felt his knee tracking in proper alignment. He bounced up and down on the stair step a few times testing out his quad muscle and it too responded well. No pain. Things felt pretty good, he thought, and he was excited to pick up the pace in the water this morning. Getting better ... back on track as it was ... no coincidences, he thought and then laughed at himself. Coincidence or related, it didn't matter; it was good to be back on track.

With dawn breaking, Andrew opened the garage, and planned his course down the mountain to Meza's training facility. The earlier he got there, the better, as training alone in a new town was something best done before the other high schoolers arrived. And if today were anything like the last two days, the orange jeep would be the first to arrive. Andrew allowed himself to recall the image imprinted in his mind; the image of the passenger in the orange jeep; a brown haired beauty with a stunning shape and a pair of suntanned legs that looked like she came right out of a model magazine.

In one deft motion, Andrew pulled the Kawasaki 125 dirt bike off the kickstand and leapt over the seat, rolling it some 100 yards out of his mom's earshot before kick starting it and gassing her up and over the gravel and sand, south down Thunderbird. Apple in his free left hand, he sat up tall on the bike, traveling down Thunderbird, out of Arroyoside Heights in the early morning dawn toward the highway. He passed the West ramp service road, then he passed the East ramp, stopping under the highway where Thunderbird dead-ended at the edge of the river. Six miles to the East ramp over the Highway, Seven miles if he went west.

From the edge of what was left of Thunderbird, he

could see the Meza Sports Complex down in the Valley. As he peered down across the river, motion caught his eye. He saw a hop and a bound, graceful sleek and lean. The bobcat then became motionless as it crouched in the brush and waited. Andrew scanned the horizon of the far bank, and became aware of the stalking Bobcat's prey. Andrew saw a black cat trapped in the thicket on the far side of the river. It's tags glimmering in the early dawn.

Like a Morse code signaling an SOS, Andrew watched the small black cat struggling to free itself. A branch from the thicket had caught the cat's harness pinning it down in the valley. Andrew shifted his gaze back over to the bobcat. The bobcat had slowly approached and was now only twenty yards away. From his perch on the riverbank, Andrew picked up a stick and threw it down at the bobcat and began throttling his engine yelling at the predator. He saw the cat roll its ears like an antenna on a radar dish, but it did not seemed concerned. A moment later, all noise became muted in the back ground as the Santa Fe thundered by back up at the railroad crossing. Lost amid the train whistle blowing and the wheels steaming on the tracks, the bobcat seemed to gain more confidence. Andrew thought the bobcat seemed to know its stealth attack was helped by the commotion of noise.

Andrew played with the throttle on his bike, measuring the width of the river, assessing the North and South banks. This side of the riverbank ended in what he saw as an excellent launch point. The riverbank on the far side looked like it was flat and that was good hard dirt; it would make a good landing zone. Andrew rolled up to the edge and looked down, studying the water and rocks. The water was shallow; rocks protruded creating pockets of turbulence in eddy currents. If he jumped and missed, the cat might not make it, but he should be able to walk across the shallow water.

"It's the fall that'll kill ya …" he recited the movie line exactly as The Sundance kid said it.

"You keep thinkin', Butch; that's what you're good at."

Sitting on the top of the crest of the hill, throttling the engine, Andrew spent a moment in contemplation, doing what he always did. He tried to visualize the flight; as if seeing it could make it so.

"Don't move until you see it," he said out loud as if studying the air out in front of him. There is a way across; all I have to do is find it. 'See it in your mind's eye,' Mr. Sebastian would say as they studied and trained together.

'There it is,' he thought! 'I see it!'

In the moment of stopped time, Andrew saw an

illuminated lattice, as if energy had organized into a physical structure, a bridge that led up and over the river safely onto the far bank. The energy lattice seemed to continue on, past the far end of the riverbank, where it disappeared into the valley below. Illuminated by a radiant light, Andrew saw the lattice glistening like the backlit gossamers of a spider's web.

"I see it Mr. Sebastian. I see the pathway. It looks like it has structure, like it is real."

Sitting on his bike, Andrew released the handbrake and gunned the throttle. He sped up the ramp and timed it perfectly. He pulled up on the handlebars as his front wheel cleared the bank, and he exploded from a crouched seated position to a standing gallop as his rear wheel left the earth. The motor whined and the wheels spun. Airborne, Andrew was flying high over the river in the thin morning air.

At the center point over the river time seemed to pause. Sounds hushed in muted tones. From the silence of his center, his aware mind took it all in, his conscious mind dormant. In that moment outside of time, in the silence, in the air floating freely, Andrew saw it all. He saw the bobcat coiled and ready to leap; he saw the black cat stuck, struggling ... sensing danger. Suspended in slow motion, beyond normal sound, he was peripherally aware of movement below him, but not concerned with it. He was aware of the background of noise, but he was enveloped in the silence of pure concentration and intense focus.

In mid flight, his awareness was called back into real-time. Andrew heard his thoughts expressed in words and he listened to his mind speaking out loud just before the jump ... "I shouldn't be doing this ... I hope I don't crash ... I should be able to make it across."

As if from within the moment itself, Andrew saw the energy lattice implode like a crystalized bridge of salt crumbling in the rain. It was as if his moment of doubt collapsed the bridge; but doubt is not real, he thought. "It has no real power, right?"

A split second later, Andrew knew he was in trouble. He felt his rear wheel moving down and to the left torqueing a bit too much he knew. He shifted his weight and began trying to correct his position. Sweat covered his forehead in nervous anticipation as his body, decelerating trough time, began to lean, adjusting his position awkwardly in midair. As he stood on air, with the nose of his bike up, and his rear wheel in midair pointing down, he tried to manipulate gravity and speed to serve his purpose. He softened his wheelbase as the ground approached him. Like landing gears on a jet, down and ready, he prepared for impact.

Andrew's rear wheel hit the dirt on the south side of the riverbed, but he lost control of the handlebars. Andrew swerved to his left, losing balance and he thrust his foot out like a rudder to compensate. With dirt squarely under his wheels, he knew he would have to release the bike and lay it down in hopes of preserving the maneuver.

Andrew let the bike slide away. A moment later he slid right behind it like a baseball runner trying to steal second base. He slid for three yards before coming to a stop and he quickly stood up, briefly looked back and headed over to his bike, which didn't look too worse for the wear. Andrew watched the bobcat take two bounds and leap away into the brush of the riverbed. Andrew hopped on the bike and headed back down to the south side of the main road, past the highway, where the black cat struggled.

"Gotcha!" Andrew shouted as he dropped his bike and clutched the black cat.

"What a find," he said to the furry friend. "And a black cat no less."

'A black cat,' Andrew thought, finding the address on the nameplate. Andrew checked the side of his leg, which was raw, and oozing a combination of blood and clear fluid like a blistering burn.

Sweat had already begun spotting his plain white V-neck tee shirt, as he held 'BlackCaz' the cat in his right arm like a football. Andrew read the address on

BlackCaz's tags and climbed up on his bike, motor still idling. He looked up at the sun and cloudless sky, and he bowed his head in a respectful nod, and with his left hand he pointed his index and long finger up as if reconnecting with the two outstretched fingers on the refrigerator door.

"Not my best landing, dad! I hope STATESIDE didn't see that!"

"Look Mr. Sebastian, a black cat ... today's glitch in the matrix," Andrew said to the sky.

"Come on BlackCaz, I better take you home."

Twenty-five minutes later, Andrew pulled into the driveway and dropped off the black cat. Mrs. Cazzie was quite apologetic, but very thankful. She offered to clean up the strawberry on Andrew's leg and gave Andrew a bottle of water that Andrew did accept just to be gracious after he had turned down a monetary reward and her invitation for breakfast.

"It was my pleasure, Mrs. Cazzie," Andrew said, "I have been wanting to jump that river now for two weeks, although a bit more gracefully maybe. BlackCaz here just gave me an excuse to finally do it...."

"Well please come by again, I'd like to introduce you to my son. I'm sure you would like him. He's a good student, and he's a running back for the football team! All State, no less!"

"Thanks," Andrew said, "I look forward to meeting him. But I've got to go now, Mrs. Cazzie, to get to my training session."

CHAPTER 6

Monday July 2, 2012

Steward Township Hospital
New Resident Orientation

07:00 AM

"The workday starts at 07:30 and please be on time. If you are going to be late, please call your teammate or text me so I will know," Grettie Trist commanded the room. Grettie, the trauma nurse coordinator had given this talk for fifteen years now, but still enjoyed ruling the roost.

"The first thing you will learn about Dr. Mackenzie is that if he thinks you are coming, he will wait … and wait … and wait. Every Kindness counts, you see, and to him it is part of the STP code of honor. So if you know you are running late, please call or text so we are not all adding hours to our day … so be prepared; know your patients; and be on time!"

"So what is STP, really," one of the new interns asked.

"STP stands for Special Treatment Program. You will understand it better as time goes on. It is an approach to patients, family, your colleagues ... a way of being, really."

"Do we need to prepare anything special for it?"

"Yes, will there be a test on it, like the boards?"

"No ... no written test. Every day life will test you enough. You'll see; you'll learn first hand how difficult it is at times ... to be courteous when patients and families are discourteous to you; to be kind when all you really want to do is attack a nurse or unit clerk ... or colleague. And in time, you will learn what compassionate caring entails. STP day in and day out is nothing special. It is employing the core values of life, day in and day out ... and believe me, Residency will be tough, as you will experience for your self, and it is easy to lose track of our prime directive and core values. STP is simply a reminder."

"The first lesson of STP and mentoring here at Steward Township Hospital residency is being courteous to your teammates. Like calling or texting if you are running late. The second principle of STP is that everyone in this building is a teammate. The third that we should cover today, is the 'being there factor.' "

"Good things happen just by showing up," Grettie announced. She looked over at Williams and recalled the first day she met him interviewing for a transitional year spot in the program at Steward Township; he travelled through an ice storm to get here on time that day. Of the thirty applicants invited to interview that day, he was one of three that braved the weather and showed up for the interview process. Dr. Mac offered him one of the positions right there and then on the spot. Being there ... and being on time ... has its advantages all right....

"So be here, on time, so we can leave on time, and you can finish on time ... or you will soon learn how easily your day expands until there is no time. No free time that is ... no time to eat, and God forbid, no time to study!"

"OK, so let's see who the lucky call team is for tonight: Dr. Eugene Simi – you are with Dr. Williams tonight. The rest of you go find your assigned residents. Good luck, learn well. I'll see ya'll in the morning. 07:30 sharp!"

———

Monday, July 2, 2012
Steward Township Hospital
Resident On-Call Room
03:00 AM

The first day of July had ended; and the first full day of the new medical year had been long. At 07:00, Dr.

Williams had rounded with Dr. Childs on all the patients they had admitted from the night before. By noon he had organized the new residents into teams, and had personally walked the new teams of residents to meet each of their Attendings. At 6 pm he started rounds on the critical ones in the ICU just before evening checkout. Dinner at 10 pm was a cafeteria hamburger and potato chips, and after four hours in the ER attending to the fallout of a motor vehicle accident, he was happy to get to the call room. He took his new resident with him, as he climbed up to the top bunk.

"Now you're sure you've got the pager to the ER?" Williams asked the new second year surgical resident. Dr. Eugene Simi's eyes were already closing on the top bunk. At five foot six inches tall, he filled three quarters of the bunk. His glasses sat on his chest, and he patted down the edges of his crisp green scrubs that were two sizes too big until his hand found the rectangular device backlight by dark green numerals.

"Yeah, I've got it," Dr. Simi responded without opening his eyes, feeling along the edge of his scrubs finding his phone, keys and then feeling the vibration of his pager when he depressed the grey button.

"And it's on ring, not vibrate, right?" Williams wasn't really asking, as he opened two mistrustful eyes now.

Dr. Simi once again found the grey switch on his

pager and slid it to bi-mode, and re-clipped it to the drawstring of his scrubs turning on the ringer.

"Bad beep is on ring and vibrate," Simi replied. "Like a belt with suspenders!" he chuckled.

"Bad beep?" Williams smirked, one eye opened now looking down from the top bunk. "Where did you get that one from?"

"Ohh, at St. Stephens, during my internship," Dr. Simi explained, "whoever was on first call was 'bad beep' because it usually meant 'no sleep'", Simi chuckled, amused by his own cleverness.

"Yeah, I understand that was a busy place," said Williams.

"We should catch a few hours of sleep while we can, no Chief?" asked Simi of the chief resident as Williams contemplated the thought of his last year of nights babysitting interns and second years while resting on a bunk in a dark closet-like call room within the basement of the hospital waiting to be summoned to the ER.

"Yes, you should get some sleep," Williams quipped, one eye hallway opening to check on the new PGY-2.

"What time do you think you ought to pre round?" Williams asked Simi a few minutes later still awake the top bunk. "How long will it take you to get caught up on our six on trauma?"

Jostled out of sleep-induced twilight of consciousness, Simi responded.

"Oh, with my ability, I need maybe five minutes for each," Simi boasted. My memory is like photogenic."

"Oh, I see. Photogenic? Well Dr. Mac is going to expect the second year residents to give a concise twenty-second synopsis of each ICU patient tomorrow, so you better be ready."

"Oh, I'll be ready alright," Dr. Simi replied to his senior resident.

"There are three patients that came in the night before you started that you haven't seen before, so leave yourself enough time to get to know them."

"Leave enough time, got it," Simi acknowledged, placing two fingers to his forehead.

"The first patient is in ICU bed-10, through and through gunshot wound to the flank; he should be able to move out of the unit if vitals are stable."

"Bed-10; shot, flank, like flank steak – in the side like a side of beef, eh, eh … no organs injured; turf him to the floor; got it," Simi acknowledged once again placing his fingers to his forehead like the Scarecrow in The Wizard of Oz, searing information into his brain for safe keeping.

"ICU-1 is TV 14406 … Motorcycle injury; air dropped in the other night; he is still on IVF, tubed, lots of facial abrasions; CT brain looked OK."

"MCA injury, road rash to face, check."

"He needs a Spontaneous Breathing Trial in another day or two, then we can wake him up."

"Bed-1; feed, breathe, wake up, got it."

"Bed-7 is also ours. He has multiple gunshot wounds; is status post splenectomy and colostomy, also still on the vent."

"Bed-7; no spleen, gut removed; another breather." Simi continued with his same process.

"There will be some consults and imaging that you will need to review; Why don't you leave yourself about fifteen minutes each so you won't have to rush," Williams directed the second year resident, "I would set the alarm for 0500."

"Are you kidding me, I've got this cold," said Simi as he tapped his forehead, and then responsibly set the time and pushed the red alarm clock numerals out of sight under the pillow next to the phone.

"5:55: locked and loaded," he said, pulling the hanging chain, extinguishing the lamp over the open paged surgical texts.

————

Monday, July 2, 2012
Intensive Care Unit
07:00

At 0700 Dr. Williams punched in the code on the keypad opening the large magnetically locked double doors gaining entrance into the ICU. He walked into the long hallway of sliding glass doors and large windowed rooms. He walked past the new shift of nurses as they broke the huddle finishing report; he avoided the frenzied worry of the surgical interns who were gathered in a huddle with their senior residents; each intern hoping to take in enough information as to not make fools of themselves in morning report.

Williams checked the trauma board that sat in front of the unit clerk but he already knew which of those beds were his responsibility as he had already gone through each earlier quickly and efficiently as Simi became bogged down chasing labs and reports within minutes after he left the call room. Glad to be early for rounds, Williams walked over to the door in front of ICU-12 first, looking unsuccessfully for pretty blue eyes set alight by a flash of red hair. But Ginny was no-where to be found. No morning coffee date today he thought.

Dr. Williams checked the monitors and dropped across the hall to the next bed on his list, ICU- bed 1. There, in a bedside chair, wearing a black habit skirted with a white band, Williams found Sister Mary Grace. Williams looked over at the nun backlit by free-floating particles suspended in the air illuminated by the streaks of sunlight pouring in from the window, as if transmitting energy from her white headband.

Jeez ... too unbelievable even for fiction, he thought, tilting his head sideways as if to allow the halo of light to take shape. Heaven let your light shine down, he thought just before making eye contact with her.

"Good morning Sister," Dr. Williams said in an animated hello to give the sister a chance to read his lips just in case she could not hear his voice. After four years as a resident seeing her almost daily, Dr. Williams still was not sure what Sister Mary Grace really could hear or see.

Sister Mary Grace looked up and said "Good morning my son," making the sign of the cross as Williams joined her in the room meeting her gaze, then adjusting her head band as if she knew Williams had been captured by it a moment before.

"Did Ginny walk you in, Sister?" Williams asked, still eye to eye with the Sister. "The nurse I mean, about this tall with red hair?" Williams added, still engaged by the Sister's blue eyes with the arc of age ringing the periphery of color.

"Yes my son, thank you," she said, still holding the stare yet to blink.

"You had her sent for me? Didn't you?" the nun asked.

"Well, no, I mean yes, it's just that I am chief as of today, and Dr. Mackenzie assigned ... no, not that ... I mean it's not as if it is an assignment ... but just making sure your needs are met … Sister … that's all."

"Thank you, Doctor, and yes, my needs are all met."

"And I agree, she is cute," said the sister with a knowing smile.

Dr. Williams just raised his eyebrows and shook his head ever so slightly. "Is it that obvious?" He asked, blushing.

"The eyes are the windows to the soul, my son."

"Yes, I've heard it said sister," Dr. Williams replied.

"Have faith … it's true," the sister said with a wink and smile. "I have it on good authority," she said pointing a finger up towards the ceiling.

"Have faith," Williams smiled. "I don't know much about faith Sister. Kinda hard sometimes to have faith when you see so much badness. Like last night; two drunk drivers injured themselves pretty severely right after we took some bullets out of two 13 year olds walking with the wrong colors; and this guy here; they think he was high on PCP before he crashed a motorcycle. God only knows what kind of mischief he was up to. He had strapped himself to a parachute probably looking for a rooftop to fly off of."

"Sounds like you made a large deposit to your grace bank account last night. You should be well pleased."

"I'm not sure I even know what a grace bank account is, Sister."

"Well last night … when you cared for and advocated for people who have lost their way and cannot choose for themselves, you became a steward of their physical lives. It is a great responsibility, and offers a great reward. A reward in the form of grace, you see."

"Grace, huh."

"Yes, every choice to help, to be of service to another brings grace to the soul. It is how we ascend, you see."

"I don't know too much about that Sister. I am just here trying to do my job. But jeez, sometimes they don't make it easy," Williams said with a hint of fatigued frustration.

Sister Mary Grace just smiled, with a deep stare into his eyes.

Despite a haze clouding the center of her eye lens, Williams felt as if the nun was once again looking right through him. He felt almost uncomfortable as if she was peering into his very essence; as if she had looked into him and came away knowing more than the shell of his exterior could tell.

"I see kindness in those eyes. I see elegance in that soul."

"Thank you sister." Williams said now uncomfortable in the moment, knowing he did not approach patient care from the same level of intention she referred to.

"Let's see what this soul is up to shall we?" Williams said as he moved past her.

Dr. Williams shifted his attention to his patient. He checked the clipboard, scanned the vital signs and looked up at the monitor. He pulled out a black stethoscope from the large pocket in his lab coat and deftly auscultated the chest and abdomen of his patient in ICU bed-1. Next, Williams undid the dressings and gently lifted each eyelid, and with a penlight he made each pupil dance. Dr. Williams gently closed each eye-lid of his sedated and paralyzed patient. He then carefully placed the pads back over TV 14406's eyes and was surprised as he saw what he recognized to be the darting eyes of a dreaming sleeper.

"I would have thought that the versed and paralytics would inhibit rapid eye movement sleep," he said out loud.

Chapter 7

The eyes of TV 14406 darted back and forth, rapidly, as Andrew Galloway climbed up on the starting block of the Meza Sports Complex stadium pool. It was 7:45 AM now and he realized he lost forty-five minutes of training time attending to BlackCaz. With only fifteen minutes or so of training time, Andrew decided on one very fast two hundred meter sprint. He smiled thinking back on all the time he and Mr. Sebastian had spent studying Ian Thorpe, and the record swim for that distance. Building fifties, each faster than the last culminating in an all-out sprint to the wall.

Andrew traveled far out over the water in Lane 3 of the Olympic sized stadium pool when in mid-air, at the apex of his dive, he saw the orange jeep appear. And despite being in mid air, he couldn't help but wonder who was in the jeep. He saw her yesterday; her form and figure branding his memory like a white-hot iron to skin.

The need to look was too much for him to fight off, and Andrew gave in, trying to catch a glimpse of the passenger in the front seat; the recesses of his mind wondering – hoping really – that she was watching him.

As Andrew's face hit the water without his chin tucked, trying to sneak a peek at her, the water ripped the goggles from his eyes. 'That's what happens when you become distracted,' Andrew said to himself. 'You make mistakes.' But Andrew could not help but become distracted. Yesterday, the passenger in the orange jeep was extraordinary.

Underwater, without his goggles, the pool of blue water was a blur. Andrew pulled up immediately wondering if the two in the orange jeep had seen the blunder. He embarrassedly swam a casual stroke and found his goggles and then coasted back to the wall of the edge of the pool, all the while eyeing the passenger in the front seat of the jeep.

'Yep, she's all that,' he thought as he climbed back up to the starting blocks. And just like yesterday, she was perfect. But, just like yesterday, she was with him; with him *again* ... and that could only mean one thing.

––––––

"He's here again," Pat Mackenzie said from behind the wheel of the orange Jeep. Pat and his female passenger sat in a two-door jeep, roll bar uncovered by the canvas top, watching the unknown six foot three inch muscular teenaged swimmer walk over to the pool. Pat, a high school senior to be, turned to the passenger in the front seat and asked, "Hey Beth, have you seen that guy around town at all?"

Beth yawned a long yawn, as if she had been jostled up out of her last five minutes of rest.

"No, can't say that I have," she said, fixing her ponytail, pretending not to notice the chiseled physique of the newcomer. Pat went on sizing up with much interest while Beth reached into her backpack and took out a bottle of sunblock and began greasing her clean, shaven legs.

"He sure looked good in the water yesterday. Someone that good has got to be here for Championships," Pat said wearing gym shorts over a training swimsuit and a sleeveless tee shirt that showed off his tan muscular arms. "What's he doing here alone, without a coach, without a team?" Pat asked from behind the wheel of the jeep, side-parted brown hair softly blowing in the Texas heat.

"Maybe he's not swimming at Championships," Beth said from the front seat, as she applied sunblock to her legs hanging over the door less cabin facing the pool with piqued interest.

"Let's see what he does in the water today," Pat said, driving the jeep around to the near side of the pool, parking by Andrew's dirt bike.

"I wonder if this is the dirt bike that Caz was chirping about," Pat said referring to his classmate who also swam for the Meza swim club and played running back for the football team. "Maybe that guy is the one who moved into the dead end west off Arroyoside heights, up by Caz's house," Pat said. "Caz said he saw someone racing a dirt bike in the mesa out the backside of the bluff up into the mountains," Pat pointed down at the dirt bike as if it were evidence.

Pat sat outside the pool in the Jeep, 30 yards from the starting block and flipped opened the stopwatch app on his phone all the while watching the athletic looking swimmer reset himself up on the starting blocks.

Andrew stood tall on the starting block and broke the seal of his goggles pretending to refit them, his green eyes searching out the passenger in the front seat. Andrew found his target, and reflexively studied the details of the lines of her swimsuit-model's body. She transfixed him as she put the backpack she was hugging down to the floor of the jeep. Andrew held his stare as her hands moved up from the floor over her head. He watched her make her windblown hair into a ponytail. Andrew took in a skin-tight one-piece red racing suit and red and white trimmed gym shorts. He noticed her auburn hair that flowed loosely, that led past her breasts to a pair of athletic, shapely tan legs. Andrew breathed in her shapely legs that were propped up on the dash of the jeep. She was the perfect combination he thought: sexy and fit. She was a super hot model-athlete.

Andrew fitted his goggles, hoping the dark blue tint would conceal his direct gaze. Safely behind the tint of his goggles on the high ground of the starting block, he watched her move. He felt his heart rate going up again, captivated by the soft curves of a physique that wanted for nothing. She pulled out a tube from her backpack and applied lotion to long muscular but feminine legs, leaving her skin glistening in the early morning sun. From behind the safety of concealment, he took in the outline of a face that he was sure was on the cover of a magazine somewhere on his mom's cocktail table.

Up on the starting block, goggles on, head up, hands on his knees, just 30 yards away, Andrew watched her head turn towards him when her actions came to a deliberate pause: it was as if she felt his eyes on her; as if she felt the weight of his stare.

In a moment of self-awareness, Andrew realized his eyes had been lingering longer than appropriate. Andrew glanced from the passenger over to the driver of the orange jeep and his eyes were met by a penetrating stare.

Sitting in the driver's seat, Pat had his phone out and ready. He waited for the swimmer to get into an athletic position but the moment was awkwardly long in coming.

"Well that didn't take long," Pat said releasing his eye lock with the swimmer and looking over at Beth with a knowing smile.

"Busted ..." Andrew breathed, embarrassed as if being caught with his hand in the cookie jar. Andrew shuddered: and his muscles turned to jelly as if poisoned by the dart of chemical shame.

"Oh great," Andrew said, quickly dropping his head down ... feeling like the engine on his bike had just stalled out.

"I should just leave now," he heard from within his own mind, as he stepped down off the blocks to reset his goggles.

"He knows I was staring, and I bet he's ticked," Andrew said to himself. And right about now he's wondering, "who is this guy – checking out *my* girl, at *my* pool!"

"And what's worse is that she knows I was staring," he thought, and he glanced quickly up to check the flash of movement as she reached to adjust the sparkle of silver dangling from her ear. Andrew's attention was called away from her as he watched the driver look down at the bike, and then flip open a cell phone in one hand.

"Great ... calling in re-enforcements," he thought.

"Time to go ..." Andrew said to himself.

Andrew wasn't sure if it was the excitement of the rescue, or the pair of legs that just kept on coming, but something inside had been ignited. He felt his heartbeat accelerate, and beads of sweat formed on his brow as his muscles relaxed. Andrew squatted down taking hold of the starting block and tested his knee and thigh. No pain. In fact, he felt pretty good. "OK, let's see what gears are available today," he thought.

Andrew looked over the water, going through his pre-game. Today's schedule should have been eight repetitions of hundred meter swims, but that was not going to happen today, he thought. The time lost from the detour with BlackCaz made him a bit too late this morning. And if his hunch was right, a throng of swimmers was likely to be here shortly.

"I probably only have time for one two hundred, today," he told himself.

"Two hundred meters in four fifties," he programmed himself, down and back, down and back.

Each distance had its appropriate pace, Andrew

knew. Flat out for fifty meters was truly that — arm turnover as fast as possible while remaining efficient in the water, legs kicking hard. Flat out for a hundred meters was not that easy, even with training. But a sprint pace for two hundred meters was nearly impossible, unless you were Ian Thorpe, the world record holder in the two hundred meter freestyle. Andrew knew the Thorpedo's splits by heart, and Andrew was on point over the first fifty; but that last one hundred and fifty was a different matter entirely. Andrew knew that the Thorpedo nearly all out sprinted the entire two hundred posting that world record time.

Andrew began to visualize his start off the block; tight entry into the water, three dolphin kicks and then pull out, no breath until the third stroke; he saw himself swim across the pool, tuck and flip at the wall, kick out, carrying the speed he needed through the finish.

"Two hundred meters paced in equal fifties," he planned. "Forget about the time," he said to himself; "it only creates pressure." It was a studied fact, Andrew knew, and a law of physics in the universe. Time is related to pressure, and focus on time takes away from immersion within the effort. In the water, Andrew would know the correct pace.

Andrew breathed in deeply, and expired slowly with controlled breath cleansing his core. He thought he was ready when his readiness was interrupted by one last thought that bubbled up from his unconscious....

"Boy," he said, "but she's really something."

Andrew entered the water with hands clasped together in a near perfect entry and streamlined kicking out nearly twenty meters past the flags over the lane ropes. Gliding effortlessly, he gobbled up distance in long powerful fists full of water.

"Wow!" said Pat as he watched the flight off the blocks, the distance in the air, the streamlined entry and depth of the dive; the leopard turned into a dolphin, with an equally impressive kick out, as powerful legs plunged together rapidly fluttering propelling him to the surface some 20 meters twenty meters past the flags over the lane ropes. Powerful arms swallowed up water and Pat knew from the stroke mechanics and the fast turnover that he was watching something special.

"This is going to be a fast hundred," he said to Beth. Pat and Beth silently watched as Andrew pulled and approached the wall completing the first hundred.

"53--!! That's crazy," Pat said, looking at his watch stopping time, counting seconds.

Andrew hit the wall at the hundred mark, tucked his head rapidly flipping and heading back to the other end, power in each kick out, an urgency in his pulls. Pat and Beth both watched Andrew finally stop the assault on the water at 200 meters.

"The second hundred seemed as fast as the first. If he was even close to the pace of that first hundred he could be … that's … no way he's like around 1:50:00! I got to talk to this guy," and Pat leapt out of the driver's side of the jeep and headed straight for Andrew.

After finishing the swim, Andrew popped off his goggles, and spot-checked his surroundings finding her gaze. He tried to press himself over the pool edge... but his effort to show off was quickly sabotaged. He quickly fell back comically into the water, too weak to muscle his way out. Instantly, his head popped up above the surface, and her giggling laugh turned his face even redder. At least she wasn't sitting there with her fingers in the shape of an L on her forehead, he thought.

Andrew waited a minute before successfully pressing his body up over the side of the pool edge landing in a squat. Although immersed by the visage of the girl in the front seat, Andrew's attention was called away to the driver of the jeep.

"Oh he's watching me looking at her …" Andrew said to himself.

The driver of the orange jeep glanced at his girl, and then stared back at Andrew. Andrew saw him hop out of the jeep, and approach him in a sprint.

"Jeez, here he comes," Andrew watched the approach. "I don't like this one bit," he said to himself, and flexed his fatigued muscles taking inventory of how much he had left in case he had to fight.

"I could run," Andrew thought. "But that wouldn't be very manly, now would it?" Andrew looked for his bike measuring the distance as he thought of options.

"I'll have to talk the driver down. 'My mom works for the school district,' he could say, 'I have the AD's permission to be here, we are new to town ... not going to be staying long.'"

But Andrew didn't have an answer for the truthful accusation of why he was so unobtrusively checking out that guy's girlfriend. Andrew couldn't rationalize that one. But he felt as if he wasn't really flirting. This seemed to be a one-way endeavor as far as he could tell.

'She probably thinks I am a dork after that flop back into the pool after my swim. And she might think I am a dork, but he will think I am a threat. He is going to feel the need to defend his girl, on his turf; and a threatened, angry ego like that will come after you.'

'He's fit, Andrew observed. And I bet he knows how to handle himself. And if today was like yesterday, the rest of his entourage will be joining him shortly. I need to play this cool, deflect him somehow, and make it out to my bike quickly.'

Apologetic candor, Andrew knew: that's what his father would have told him: Apologetic candor goes a long way in situations such as this.

Andrew dried his legs off on the deck, careful to protect his strawberry-skinned thigh. Head up, forward, posture flexed like a football player, Andrew prepared for contact.

"Better to stay low at first," he told himself, and he braced himself for impact.

A pair of muscular legs that looked like they belonged to a football player stopped in front of Andrew. Andrew heard a "Hey ... " followed by a long pause.

Andrew rose up from drying off his legs, eye to eye with the jealous boyfriend, waiting for the rest of the greeting to follow. Expecting to hear 'hey ... what are you doing checking out my girlfriend,' Andrew took a moment to see what he was up against. An inch shorter than Andrew, with hazel eyes, he was clean-shaven and suntanned. He looked like a warrior, Andrew thought, and he looked like he knew how to handle himself.

"How you doing?" ... The driver extended a hand. "Pat," and Andrew received an open extended palm with a firm grip.

"Hey," Andrew replied noncommittally, tensing up ready ... "I'm Andrew; Andrew Galloway," he said thinking it a bit strange. Andrew did not expect a greeting, let alone a handshake. Oddly, Pat seemed excited not angry.

A moment later, a second silhouette materialized in form. Even though he didn't want to, Andrew could not help but become captured by her. She was simply stunning, he thought. She had long hair, and up close her eyes seemed soft. Her tanned skin was smooth and as she approached, Andrew could not help but notice the sexiest walk he could ever imagine. Sexy without trying, it seemed to him. Probably King and Queen at the prom, Andrew thought as he forced himself to take his eyes off her.

"Hey, what is your best time for a hundred?" Pat asked, still excited.

"What?" Andrew replied, puzzled, still waiting for a fight. Andrew paused, centering himself, not expecting that type of question. He was expecting something like, 'hey, how you doing, you know this is our club our pool, and by the way, take your foreign eyes off her she with me….'

"For a hundred!" Pat went on. "How fast can you go?"

Andrew put down his guard, slightly, trying to center himself, allowing the question to penetrate his consciousness.

"For a hundred? Meter? You mean swimming?"

"Yeah, swimming," Pat laughed amusedly. "The hundred meter free. How fast can you go?"

"Not sure," Andrew replied, his shocked mind drifting in a new direction now.

Andrew knew Mr. Mendonhall could easily recite the series of slower and slower splits that Andrew had recently turned in.

"What! Not sure? That's crazy!"

"I haven't swam for time in a while now," Andrew said collecting himself. And besides, I've been mostly working up to two hundreds," he said.

"Two hundreds? Are you swimming the two hundred in the meet tomorrow?"

"What?"

"You're swimming here tomorrow, right? At Championships?" Pat asked.

Andrew eased up a bit more. This Pat guy didn't seem angry at all.

"No, I am just training," Andrew replied using all his concentration and effort to keep eyes locked on Pat, but intensely aware of the near irresistible magnetic pull towards her.

"That's crazy! Who do you swim for," Pat asked again.

"Whom do I swim for?" Andrew repeated, allowing himself to catch a quick glimpse of her out of the corner of his eye.

"My father," Andrew replied seriously.

"I know what you mean" ... Pat chuckled. "But really; who do you swim for? What club?"

"No, I mean I train with my father ... no club, no competitions ... just training, you know?" Andrew stood eye-to-eye with Pat, trying hard not to stare at his girlfriend. Pat saw Andrew's distracted glance even as he tried to hide it.

"Oh, this is Beth," Pat offered, giving Andrew a legitimate reason to meet her eye to eye.

"Hi both, nice to meet Beth of you ... Beth of you, I mean both." Andrew extended his hand again to Pat, and then pulled it back, then put it out again, to shake hands with Beth who never moved, but put on a quizzical face as she watched him become red-faced and flustered.

Beth smiled, and caught his confused hand with hers, as Andrew went away. In that moment of eye contact, with a 'hello' that came in an ordinary moment in a new city on an ordinary day of the week, Andrew stopped breathing and paused, as he became absorbed with her. Andrew, frozen in the moment, breathlessly took her all in. He moved from her eyes, pretty and brown; to her hair that she had pulled back away from her face, to her lips, perfectly formed in an inviting smile; to her form of youthful curves with legs that take shape from work and effort. It was unlike any moment he had experienced before as he was captivated by all of her, as if he was meeting a celestial being that attracted him like a paperclip to a magnet; a pull so strong, he could not let go of her hand.

Beth smiled more fully as she looked into his pretty green eyes as Andrew kept her hand; she had seen other guys look at her before the same way ... and she smiled a coy smile, looking into highlight green eyes knowing that he was hooked; but for the moment, that was OK. Beth felt a sincerity within the comical, tongue-tied, boy-man in front of her and that was OK too.

"Nice to meet you too," Beth laughed and took back her hand.

"Well I got you at 53 seconds for a hundred meters," Pat said, "that's probably fast enough to win the hundred here tomorrow at Championships. And, if any of the scouts see you post that kind of time, a swim like that will and land you a D-1 scholarship. That's faster than the best swimmer around here. And Levine, the guy who set the mark last year, is probably going to get an invite to swim in California. If you go that fast, that could be you! And I don't think you slowed down on the second hundred. That's crazy!"

Andrew collected himself from his visage of Beth, and shifted his weight side to side, back on guard, but Pat seemed more concerned with swimming details, than about the girl.

"Yeah, well I don't think that is for me," Andrew said looking at Pat but unable to stop himself from glancing back over to Beth. Andrew reddened as Beth met his eyes with a smile. Beth turned her head slightly to the side, smiling, leaving Andrew in a full on blush. Andrew collected himself quickly and escaped by looking down and away and then refocusing on Pat who was poised with another question.

"You must have swum club before?" Pat asked.

"Oh, you know, I swam competitively for a while … but not now, you know how it goes," Andrew answered dodging the question and feeling more relaxed. Pat was definitely more interested in swimming than fighting.

Andrew struggled to stay locked in, as a part of his brain wanted to take him back to her. He tried to stay focused on Pat, but momentarily lost the train of conversation, as he could not help himself any longer. His eyes were drawn back to her, and she met his glance with the same deep penetrating response, allowing his eyes to linger on her, hands on her hips weight shifted to one side, allowing him to see her. Andrew's eyes lingered on Beth a moment longer than he would have wanted to, and in that moment, he knew that she knew.

"Well you look fitty pat yourself," Andrew said to the two of them, trying to regain some kind of composure, still unnerved by the assault on his energy; an assault from a fight that didn't materialize and a spark that held his thoughts jumbled.

"That's because he's Pat," she said, again smiling a playful but deep smile as if daring him to process her presence. Beth shifting the weight of her backpack over her hip, unable to resist walking Andrew down the road just a bit further into embarrassment.

"How did you do?" asked Pat.

"What's that," Andrew glanced back over from Beth to concentrate on Pat.

"In club … how did you do … racing?"

"I did OK when I was a junior," Andrew offered, without details.

"Why did you stop competing," Pat asked, incredulously.

"Oh, I don't know, you know how its gets," he replied, reliving the inner torment that comes with the experience of a bad coaching match up, and the loss of fun. Not to mention the expectations associated with winning, and the demons of pressure.

"Now I just mostly train."

"That swim was too fast to just be training. How did you get this good?" asked Pat.

"Ah, you know … its one of those things … to go fast, you have to stop trying to go fast, and just move into the space of being fast," Andrew recited as if from wrote memory.

"What? Is that some kind of Samurai thing?"

Andrew realized he was looking like more of an oddity than he must already appear to be.

"Oh, you know, just something I worked on with an old coach of mine."

"Someone is coaching you then," stated Pat, with even more interest.

"Well I usually train with my father, but he's away on a mission right now." Andrew said, flashing back to the surreal moment of connection of two fingers and a very much-missed father.

"Military?" Pat asked.

"Well sort of ... STATESIDE is private agency that works closely with the military. He got pulled to a deployment op a few days after we moved here. I've been training alone over the last two weeks now," Andrew relaxed a bit, feeling confident that this meeting was not about Andrew invading his pool or his girlfriend.

"I thought you must be new to town. That you riding the Mesa out West of town?"

"Yes, we live up Thunderbird in a cul-de-sac that backs up to the mesa. Pretty good for riding and jumping," Andrew offered, more relaxed now, clearly no fight in the cards here, and if he just kept his eyes off of her he was able to remain dialed in to the conversation.

"Well, Regional Championships are here tomorrow

— the best from the southwest will be here competing. Post a time like the one I just got you at, and you could get an invite to swim at the next level."

"Oh, really ..." Andrew looked back over at the two of them, briefly taking in Pat's athletic physique next to the tall, tan, curvy figure of Pat's knockout girlfriend.

"Have you committed yet?"

"What," Andrew asked incredulously, his mind darting to the unsigned commitment papers for Annapolis on his desk upstairs....

"Are you going to swim in college? Do you have any offers from colleges yet?"

"Oh, no, I am not planning on swimming in college. I'm more interested in flight school, you know. I have a few things I'm considering, but I'm not locked into anything yet," Andrew offered evasively. Andrew's mind flashed to the paperwork for Annapolis and a military career, which was on top of his desk, waiting for completion, and the application to the STATESIDE Cadet Training program, all but completed, and safely buried deep in his bottom drawer.

"Still battling ... head against heart, you know."

The application for the cadet-training program at STATESIDE was ready to go. Andrew hid the completed application below Sheldrake's treatise on Morphogenetic Fields Theory or M-Fields. While the chances that his heart's desire would leak out and be discovered by his mother or father were slim, he wanted to play his hand close to the vest. The completed application should be safe, there, he thought.

Andrew knew The Naval Academy was an exceptional opportunity, and had a lot to offer all right... but his heart was with STATESIDE. But thinking it was the easy part. Saying it out loud, when it counted, that was the tough part. And as of yet, he had not said it out loud to any one.

"Well there will be a ton of colleges here tomorrow" Pat finished. "You should come check it out...."

With his attention back on Beth, Andrew remained lost in thought for a moment, looking full on at her. Pretty face, warm brown eyes, flowing hair, muscularly feminine body.... Wow ... he thought.

"So what do you think?"

"I think she's amazing," Andrew said reflexively then immediately blushed, too late to take back the words he heard come out of his own mouth. Andrew caught himself quickly, "I mean I think that's amazing, tomorrow, all the excitement, the big meet."

Idiot ... Andrew thought to himself, hoping neither caught his blunder.

Pat saw Andrew's eyes break away from Beth, and Beth let his gaze go, shaking her head slightly and laughing with an amused and flattered smile.

'Thank God neither of them seemed offended or embarrassed. I bet she must be used to it,' Andrew thought.

"And it's here tomorrow?"

"Yep...."

"Are you both swimming?" Andrew bravely directed his question to her.

'Of course she's swimming,' he thought, 'why else would she be here in racing suit training with her boyfriend?' Andrew felt his face flush red again.

"Yep," Pat answered for them both. "We swim for Meza Swim Club ... most of us go to school together."

"Well, I may stay and watch for a bit ... I plan on getting here a bit earlier to train tomorrow morning," he replied to Beth after a quick glance at Pat.

"Come to think of it, my mom said something about working the event tomorrow. She was just hired by the school district," Andrew said, finally getting back to some of his rehearsed strategy.

"Great," Pat broke through, "meet starts at 10 AM. You are welcome to stay and train with us today if you like. We are tapering so it will be a short work-out; starts and turns, form and speed ..." he said.

Before Andrew could reply, the first pack of followers unloaded out of a pick-up behind him. Pat's conversation with Andrew was interrupted by a palm to palm high five greeting....

"What's up Pat?" Caz shot out.

"Mornin' sunshine!" Caz tried to reach up and protectively pull Beth in under his arm like a familiar friend protecting his own. Beth was quick enough to avoid being bear hugged by Caz, and fended him off with her backpack resourcefully using it like a shield.

"Who's this?" Caz tilted his head up and puffing out his chest, aware of his gymnastic type of build, and shorter stature compared to Pat and the taller and well-proportioned physique of Andrew. Caz stepped back and squinted his eyes noticing the strawberry on Andrew's thigh.

"What'd ya scrape the side of the pool this morning? You should really use the ladder, rook."

"Thomas Cazzie," Pat introduced, "this is Andrew Galloway."

"Hey," Andrew offered extending his hand, "I think I might have met your mom this morning; don't happen to own a black cat by any chance do you?"

"Andrew's new to the area, Caz, in fact he lives up by you."

"Oh, yeah?" Caz glanced over to Andrew's bike, and said; "Now someone 'new to the area' has been out riding in the Mesa kicking up dust all over my truck. Do you know something about that?"

Back on guard, Andrew released Caz's hand with a menacing feeling that said 'danger'; New town, new traps ... he thought.

A few moments later, the parking lot received a few more pick-ups and jeeps. Andrew saw the rest of the team heading straight for Pat, and he knew he best be off.

"When outmanned and underequipped, evade ..." he told himself drifting to Sun Tzu's treatise on The Art of War.

"I've got to get going...." Andrew picked up his gear; glad his jelly legs had recovered. "It was good to meet you both," he said respectfully to Beth, who couldn't hold back another chuckle. Andrew then acknowledged Pat and said, "Thanks for the invite. Good Luck tomorrow." After glancing quickly past them he stepped around Caz, and said, "good to met you, Tom."

"Good to meet you rook."

Andrew packed up his gym bag, slid into his jeans and headed out toward the parking lot. He threw his leg over the bike and kick started it up, circling back around one more time, before racing away back up to Thunderbird.

Andrew rode up Thunderbird, back towards the house, heart still pounding at a fast pace, thoughts racing even faster.

'Caz was not quite as cool as his mom,' he thought.

'But at least there was no fight. I should sign those papers and report to STATESIDE September 1st,' Andrew thought as he shifted gears and headed up to the Mesa to Arroyoside heights. 'But boy, she's all that,' he couldn't help himself.

CHAPTER 8

July 2, 2012
Steward Township Hospital
ICU
0720

"It looks like he is in rapid eye movement sleep," Williams explained to the non-medical nun; "so we know he has some brain function, and that is a good sign. As for his soul – well that's just impossible to know, isn't it?"

"Yes, the journey of the soul is quite the mystery. I have found that one best goes about it day by day."

"And what about his face; all that swelling?"

"Those facial abrasions tend to weep; but they should heal over time. Those facial abrasions – we call it road rash Sister."

"Road rash, yes I see."

Dr. Williams saw the sister's eyes move toward the blue tube exiting the patient's mouth, and attached to the breathing machine.

"He was already intubated when he landed … in other words he arrived with the tube already in, Sister."

"He'll be on the vent for at least a few days," Williams pointed over to the big box like piece of equipment that pushed the air of life into the patient's rising and falling chest. "If his numbers look good we will give him a breathing trial; see how his chest is rising and falling in a steady rhythm and his heart is in a sinus rhythm – those are good things."

"See that; every cloud has its silver lining."

"Are you able to see the tracing on the monitor Sister? Are you able to see the vital signs of life?"

"Well, my eyes are dulled and old, and I don't see those many things. But I do see the signs of vital life. I see two of God's children, each meeting by an appointment set by destiny."

"Well he is my assignment Sister. He didn't exactly make an appointment, trust me on that. In fact, he dropped in rather unexpectedly."

"Yes, the unexpected can test us … give us an idea of what we are, what we have become."

"I was here last night when he arrived; under very mysterious circumstances, I might add, Sister."

"Ahh, see that?"

"What's that Sister?"

"Mystery … it has its roots in mysticism, and to me

that means the hand of God brought him here. Here as if by appointment to meet you."

"To meet me? I'm not so sure about that Sister. I'm pretty sure some sort of accident brought him here, Sister."

"The Divine works in mysterious ways, my son. Events are orchestrated in ways we don't understand for reasons we don't understand."

"I don't know Sister. After four years of this, I think bad things happen because they just do. No rhyme of reason … they just do."

"All things are revealed in God's time, my son. I am sure he is here for a reason; probably a reason that we do not understand with our limited perception."

Williams auscultated the chest of his patient, listening to the heart beating regularly and saw the rhythm trace a dancing pattern across the monitor. Williams had been at Steward Township Hospital over four years now, and there was not a day he could remember where he did not see the Sister somewhere in the ICU. With his ears plugged by his stethoscope, he saw Sister Mary Grace's mouth moving, and he knew she was singing. He had heard her singing often and he had ben impressed by the sweetness of her voice. Williams listened for a moment, the background song resonating beautifully as the chest of his patient rose, and the fell again, and the heart of his patient skipped in a regular rhythm, tracing a recording on the monitor above. The song was a familiar one, and Williams filtered out the sounds of life, as the Sister sang:

Make me a channel of your peace.

Where there is hatred let me bring your love.

Where there is injury, your pardon,

And where there is doubt true faith.

O master grant that I may never seek

So much to be consoled as to console

To be understood, as to understand,

To be loved as to love with all my soul.

For it is in giving that we receive,

In pardoning that we are pardoned

And in dying that we are born to eternal life.

Williams unplugged from his auscultation and stared deeply into the hazy eyes of the seventy plus year old nun who wore a familiar black habit, black head dress with a white band. Despite her age, Williams felt a vibrant energy about her. It seemed as if an energy, like a beam of light from a flashlight, was transmitted to the patient she sang to. He placed his stethoscope back in his pocket and stepped back from the bedside.

"Please go on, Sister. With the song I mean. You have a beautiful voice."

"Oh, stop now young man..." Sister said with a coy

smile. I don't want that pretty nurse jealous of me!"

Williams laughed, and hummed the first verse of the song of prayer that Sister Mary Grace had been singing.

"Do you think prayer helps, Sister? I mean can it really make a difference?"

"Yes. Yes I do. And yes ... yes I believe it can."

"How so, Sister?"

"Although prayer seems insignificant in the face of such grave medical occurrences, I believe that God responds."

"You believe that God actually answers some prayers for help?"

"I believe that God responds to all prayers ... but not in the way you are thinking. Prayers are not granted in a literal way. There is no manipulating God, you see. Too powerful for that I am afraid."

"So if not in a literal way are prayers answered in some other way?"

"Well, most people are asking for a specific out-come. Like to get well ... but a prayer that includes sur-render to God's will, well that can be can be quite pow-erful. Transformative even."

"So we shouldn't pray for our patients to get better?"

"If we pray for the highest good of each soul, then we are praying in concert with the power of the Holy Spirit. Prayer that is integrous, like a prayer for the highest good, can have a positive effect over time. The highest good you see … it is what you should pray for."

"The highest good, humph. I'll have to think about that one. Is that why you choose to sing The Prayer of St. Francis?" Williams asked, as he remembered his evenings at Saturday night services back home – a memory that seemed to be from a lifetime ago.

"Yes, The Prayer of Saint Francis … very good," she said, "you know it. The Prayer of St. Francis is one of my favorites."

"Why is that?"

"Well I believe that God works through the people in the world. So I pray to be a vessel, or a channel of Peace. I pray to be what you already are, my son."

"What I am?"

"Yes, what you are. A vessel, an instrument of the lord; helping those at a time when they cannot help themselves."

"Thank You Sister, you are kind to say that, but I don't feel that way. I am just doing my job."

"Yes, you may think you are doing your job, but I tell you that you and I are not very different."

"Why do you say that Sister?"

"We are each here by appointment. We each meet many souls on a sacred journey; some of whom have found a little trouble along the way perhaps, but souls that need our help. Remember, The good things we do for any other is of great spiritual merit."

"Grace," Williams said out loud as if response to her comment.

"Yes?" said the sister as if responding to her name.

"Oh, no Sister, I wouldn't presume to call you 'Grace' I was referring to what you had said earlier, you know, well anyway, well, trouble is what I'll be in if I don't move on, sister," Williams said as he checked his watch and scanned the monitors one last time before folding his stethoscope into the back pocket of his scrubs.

"Thanks for the kind words, sister," Williams said before leaving.

"Every kindness counts, my son," he heard as he walked out as song once again graced the air.

———

July 2, 2012
Steward Township Hospital ICU
0720

"Ten minutes left, and I've got to get through the rest of the ICU," Simi remarked. Outside ICU-1, Simi flipped the chart cabinet down with a loud metallic screech. He could see his patient lying still, undisturbed by the screeching noise. He opened the chart up to the orders section and peered into the room through the glass window and looked around.

"Let's see what we're dealing with," he said looking through the window from the hallway.

Peering into the room beyond the glass, he did a double take as he saw the occupant in robe and habit, sitting in the bedside chair.

"What the...? She shouldn't be here!" Simi checked his watch, which only reminded him how pressed for time he had become. It's too early for visitors. "She's going to have to wait outside," he said to the glass window.

Simi watched the nun sitting in the bedside chair holding hands with his motionless patient in ICU-1. Simi listened with disgust as she began singing.

"Make me a channel of your peace ..." he heard, "where there is hatred let me bring your love ... "

Simi stood outside the room, studying the electronic data that floated across the screens like a scoreboard, and jotting down the key elements of the patient in ICU-1, as the sister sang on. While working, Simi unconsciously began clutching repeatedly to hike his green scrub pants that kept drooping by the weight of a pager, a phone, and a safety pin holding keys and a watch. His medium length white lab coat was stuffed with a stethoscope, a reflex hammer, how-to manuals and pages of to be completed progress notes. While Simi flipped through the chart, going through the medical records, he watched and listened. His patient was looking away from him, away from the hallway window, toward a tray table near the only outside window in the room. Adjacent to the outside window was a small portable tray table, with some clothes folded sitting on the table. Simi watched the nun end her song of prayer and walk around to the tray table, as if to see what the patient was looking at. Simi's eyes followed the Sister to the far side of the room, where the Sister picked up a Polaroid photo that was propped on the clothes folded on the tray table. With a chuckle, the sister laughed, and said, "Can't take your eyes off of her, I see."

Simi peered into the room to see whom the sister was speaking to. The sister seemed to be looking straight at the patient in the bed. Simi leaned forward inspecting the back of the room to be sure the nurse was not in the back of the room charting. Nope: no one there, he noted. Simi saw the Sister continue talking, as if she were having a conversation with the lifeless, intubated, sedated trauma victim.

"Ah, I can see it in your eyes," Simi heard her say to the patient. "You loved her from the moment you saw her, didn't you my son?"

"I hope you are not waiting for a reply, sister," Simi mumbled under his breath.

And no sooner than he had finished his chuckle, Simi's pager went off. Before he could react, the vibration of the pager overcame the drawstring on his scrub bottoms. Dr. Simi's scrub bottoms collapsed to the floor sending his pager left, his phone right and his keys directly in front of him. With the white skin and wire-like hair of his legs exposed Dr. Simi reached down to his short white ankle socks quickly collecting his green scrubs that had gathered in a pile on the floor.

As the first responder to the scene, Ginny broke out in laughter at the sight of a pair of bare, hairy, pale legs that appeared below the bottom of a white lab coat, while his green scrub bottoms kissed the floor. When the resident emerged upright again Ginny saw his face as red as a beet.

"You all right?" she asked pausing to catch the name on his picture ID, "Dr. Simi is it?"

"You have him, right?" Simi deflected a bit flustered as he tried to divert attention and escape the humiliation unscathed.

"I need all the labs printed out," Simi tried to inconspicuously loop his keys and watch back onto his scrubs, and secure his beeper and phone. "And the radiology reports? Where are the radiology reports? I can't find any of the reports? And what's up with the nun? Shouldn't she be waiting outside until visiting hours begin? Come on now, I've got work to do and this is taking too long ..." he panicked checking his watch secured to his scrubs by an oversized safety pin. "Rounds start in like five minutes. And she needs to wait outside. Visiting hours are like in ninety minutes," he finished.

Without waiting for answers Simi lumbered around Sister Mary Grace, noticing a slight haze in her right eye.

"Cataract no doubt," he diagnosed, passing the sister.

Simi scrunched his brow and glanced off ... and then fumbled with his reflex hammer that became tangled in his stethoscope before he began auscultating and percussing the chest of TV 14406 in ICU-1. He emerged from the room and once again engaged Ginny.

"Who's the nun," Simi asked again, pointing to Sister Mary Grace, his ears still blocked by two long black tubes attached to the diaphragm of his stethoscope.

"First day," Ginny asked the resident as he took the stethoscope out from his ears.

"Who me, oh, no, no. Not really, I mean yes, this is my first rotation on T-1, first day on Dr. MacKenzie's service, but I'm a second year, finished my internship at St. Stephen's where we were twice as busy as this. You'll probably hear me reporting later on in rounds ... so I'm going to go through his chart for a minute then I'll let you know if I have any new orders for you OK?"

"Yes sir," Ginny said, amusedly, "just let me know."

Ginny pressed 'print' on the wall side monitor and picked up the labs and radiology reports off the printer.

"Here you go," she said to Dr. Simi.

Ginny went inside the room, and smiled at Sister Mary Grace, and checked on her patient. Dr. Simi followed Ginny back in to the room and spoke as if the sister wasn't even there. "Who's the nun?" he asked pointing to Sister Mary Grace who was saying prayers while holding the hand of the patient in ICU-1.

"This is Sister Mary Grace, 'Dr.' Simi, from Grace of Souls – that is the convent attached to the hospital," Ginny pointed to the other side of the breezeway – a tube that connected a convent building with the hospital. "She will not get in your way, I promise. Think of her as a special part of Dr. MacKenzie's team."

"Oh, you mean like she's trained in palliative care? Death and dying and all that? Well don't take this one yet sister, he's only been here a few days. I've barely got my hands on him for the save."

"I think you have got her confused with the grim reaper," Ginny smiled looking pleasantly at the sister, who gave Ginny an approving wink at the quip. Sister Mary Grace then just smiled at them both, gazing deeply into each of their eyes in alternating engagements.

"Yes, my son. I like to think I work for the other side," she said to the young doctor.

Ginny smiled, "that's right Sister. Heaven help us."

"Sister Mary Grace ... I see, yes ... Dr. Mackenzie you say eh ..." Simi said pondering. "OK, I guess she can stay. But be careful that she doesn't touch any of the wires – this is all very sophisticated equipment!"

"Will do, sir," Ginny said sarcastically throwing up a salute, as she walked out to the window overlooking the inside of ICU-1.

"I'm going to have to keep an eye on that one," she said to herself from behind the window.

"She's cute," said Dr. Simi to the poor-sighted nun, "I might have to ask her out."

————

0725

Dr. Jason Williams spotted Ginny as she sat at the outside window looking into the room of her post, guarding the trauma patient in ICU-1. He offered her a familiar smile as he approached, and walked up to her calling her attention to him from her charting.

"Good morning, Ginny."

"Hey, there. Good Morning yourself."

"Thanks for walking Sister Mary Grace in this morning," Dr. Williams said to the nurse, absorbed in her blue eyes.

"No problem. Happy to do it," she replied.

"So; any new changes?"

"No, not really," she said, "night shift reported that he had been quiet overnight, satting 93%, heart rate blood pressures stable, sedated on the vent."

"Alive, but not awake," she interjected matter-of-factly.

"I know many people alive but not awake," chuckled Dr. Williams, and they are not paralyzed, sedated, on the vent! Just wait until you meet my new second year!"

"Just had the pleasure," Ginny laughed, brushing him on the shoulder.

"Do you mind paging me if anything comes back?" Dr. Williams asked her.

"Sure," said Ginny. "I'd be happy to call you."

Williams' pager went off and Ginny could see that Dr. Williams was lost in the possibilities of the message. She let him disengage from the dialogue and she walked out of the room to the chart station window. "Sorry," Dr. Williams said coming to find her, "I'll check back in with you in a little bit. We'll be back over for rounds report at 7:30."

"It's a date," Ginny quipped back.

"Ahh … you liked him from the moment you saw him," said sister Mary Grace from the bedside chair looking at the Polaroid while eavesdropping on the conversation behind her.

"I did, TV 14406 responded to the ether. I liked her from the moment I saw her. That's why I had to go the next day. I went there to see her."

CHAPTER 9

August 27 2004

Meza, Texas

The red numerals flashed as the chime alarm sounded and Andrew woke up. Andrew reset the clock next to his bedside, unplugged his phone from the charger, and began his morning.

He stuffed his goggles into his Backpack along with a drag suit for training and slipped into his cutoff blue jeans. He pulled on a clean soft gray cotton T-shirt and then rifled through his top drawer grabbing a comb that he threw into his backpack. He stared down a small sample bottle of Ralph Lauren, but he just walked by it.

Andrew started his running and swimming workout well before the crowd started to fill the Sports complex parking lot. By the time he had finished, the entrance was blocked off and he had to walk around the

111

stadium to get access to the hospitality tent where his mother would be working.

As Andrew walked around the stadium parking lot, the sight was a familiar one; cars coming in, single file, with big white lettering and club logos decorating the dark tint of the rear windows of the vehicles with the names of the swimmers listed below.

San Antonio Swim club; Bentonville High Arkansas State Champs, Catholic Elite; Longhorn Aquatics Speed; Lake Travis Senior High Swim Club; Cavaliers Swim; East Texas Summer Swim Club; Alamo Area Swim Association; Dallas Mustangs; Texas ATAC; Coronado High School Swimming. Champs and stars from Arizona, New Mexico and Texas were well represented. Andrew smiled remembering with some nostalgia his start in summer swimming. He couldn't help notice the feeling of innocence that accompanied that nostalgia, back in the day when swimming was fun and full of promise.

Andrew began walking on when he stopped in front of a back of a white Suburban, and paused. Its limousine-tinted rear window brandished a logo that said up "The Torpedoes."

Andrew paused in reflection; "Go get'em Thorpey," he said, and couldn't help notice the bump in his heart rate and the tightness in his chest as his body responded immediately to the memory of competitive swimming two levels past what was to be today.

The crowd of five hundred eventually became two thousand as the buses and cars arrived for the Ten AM start of the Championships. Experienced parents, grandparents and siblings gathered in the bleachers of the indoor-outdoor stadium-like complex. They spread their blankets over the bleachers, propped up bleacher pads for comfort and unzipped the thermo seal food bags hunkering down for the event. Andrew walked past the backside bottom of the stadium where meet officials generated heet sheets, posting times and seedings on the wall.

When he arrived at guest services, Andrew found his mother with a walkie-talkie in one hand and a Polaroid camera hanging around her neck. She was sorting photo ID's and attaching them to credentials all the while directing traffic on behalf of the School district, hosting the event.

"Hi dear," she said with a warm smile.

"Mom, you are not seriously using that old relic for work are you? Why don't you use the digital camera?"

"Hummmm," she smiled a chuckle, "sometimes old tech is good tech. Point and click, and ... voilà ... and best of all, it's an Instamatic!" Andrew heard the gears unwind from the back of the camera after the flash lit up his face, and the next thing he knew his mom was waving wet cardboard film back and forth, air-drying the emerging image. True to form, when he least expected it, there was mom snapping a picture – no doubt another post to the over-run refrigerator.

Andrew stayed near his mother who left the hospitality tent to check on the patrons in college row. The coats hung over the chairs read, Stanford, Cal, USC, UCLA, Texas, UA, Baylor and smaller schools in the west, Midwest.

'Maybe I was wrong,' he thought. 'Maybe not just some B level summer swim meet. Must be some good swimmers here today if these schools are recruiting,' Andrew thought. 'The Division One schools will be looking for fast times, and the best swimmers: Swimmers who are not afraid to compete,' he thought feeling a surge of adrenaline.

Andrew moved on past college row to find his mother in the 'Staff Only' section of the bleachers. "Impressive turnout huh?" She said referring to college row. "But no 'Go Navy' banners anywhere to be seen," she said pointing to the absent flag of The Naval Academy.

"I think that's an East Coast thing. This is a Texas thing."

"You'd think that the U.S. Naval Academy could use a few good Texas swimmers!" She said.

"No surprise," Andrew said. "If there is one thing I have learned in the last few weeks it's that Texas is like no other country," he said.

Andrew became quiet again scanning the pool deck for a pair of long tan legs.

"Any regrets?" Andrew's mother asked him compassionately, interested.

"What, walking away?" he turned to her, eye to eye, to check the nonverbal tenor of her question. He realized she was honestly interested in his feelings, not pushing her own agenda.

"Not really," Andrew said. "I am happy to have left racing behind."

"You must have been under a lot of pressure, dear."

And with nothing more than the thought of racing, Andrew felt his chest tighten, while his heart rate ticked up; the nervous energy produced the sensation of nausea – Butterflies, the coaches called them: a reflex physiological response to the tension of the moment.

Andrew looked up into the stands, and watched the swimmers in warm-up and couldn't help but feel nauseous. The nausea, he realized came partly from knowing you were about to push your body all out. But the nausea came also from the risk: the risk to your own self.

Andrew knew that every time he stepped up on the blocks he risked exposing what he was made of: what his heart looks like, what his strength of will looks like; and that was scary. Especially when your mind held doubt. Doubt. Doubt, and Fear: two demons that seemed to be always lurking in the background, testing you with each swim: demons that can take over your mind and weaken your physical body, rendering you powerless to compete. And when you begin to believe that you don't have what it takes, the demons win. It is all in the mind and Andrew knew that mindset first hand, in California. In California, he had lost the art of no-mind, of the quiet mind. He walked away with doubt and fear that reflexively, returned, here and now.

Relax, he told himself. Relax and just watch. You don't have to compete.

"You know if any of them saw you swim they would be printing scholarship papers right here," she said pointing to college row. "I bet you can make any of those teams if you wanted."

"Thanks mom, he said." But Andrew thought otherwise.

"I don't know Andrew. I am sure Annapolis would gladly take you – even as a walk on," Andrew's mother replied.

"Thanks, but no thanks. Now if any of those coaches want to start a dirt-bike team, then I'm their man," he said.

"Yes, well I can't wait for you to put that bike up ... she said with hope. "As an officer, in the Navy, you won't need to jump motorcycles."

"It's a dirt bike Mrs. Galloway," Andrew ignored her plug for the military academy.

"As an officer, you'll need a respectable vehicle," she replied. "Why don't we get you a car for your birthday, so you can get around like a normal senior."

"Thanks, but I'll hold out until I have my pilot's license. Then we can talk about airworthy transportation. And besides, you never know; handling a bike well just might come in handy. Dad told me most of the time the scouts on reconnaissance move over ground on dirt bikes ... it's good to have those skills, I'll be a real asset to the company," he chided.

Amanda cringed at the thought.

"Impossible! You and your father are just alike!" she exclaimed.

"You know there's a lot more to do in the Navy other than fly off the back of a moving ship!"

"Well, what can I say ... I want to be all I can be!"

"Why Andrew Galloway, did you hear what you just said?"

"Oops. Sorry. It's not just a job it's and adventure?"

Amanda reflected on the irony – Her husband travelling the world setting up air evacuation programs.

And even though he told her he was far away from the conflict, she knew better. She knew he still piloted some of those helicopters – helo's he called them – and traveled to field sites dropping in to the men on the ground. She cringed at the thought of grenades, explosions, and IED's going off around him in some parts of the world where human life was the cost of doing business.

Andrew stood with his mother, staring out facing the pool in a contemplative pause. And, staring at her son, as if reading the radiating waves of energy floating off him as he gazed out over the pool, she cringed a second time at a new thought. Maybe it was mother's intuition, but she got the feeling her son was planning on a career that included piloting, but not through the Naval Academy.

"I couldn't get dad on his mobile again this morning before I left for workout. Did he say anything before he left again last night?" he asked.

"No, I tried his cell, too, but it went right to voice mail. He might be up, but who really knows where he is … there may not even be cell service where he is."

Yes, that was both the thrill and the danger, Andrew realized. STATESIDE took teams out to remote parts of the world: out near the 'theater of operations'. They were in Afghanistan, Korea, and all over Canada and Europe working with both the military and civilian companies on air evacuation. It was at times dangerous, but no doubt necessary.

At breakfast some mornings, Andrew heard his mom coaxing his father to step down from the operations end of the business; step down from fieldwork. Although he didn't tell her, she knew that he at times he still piloted ground to base rescue. She tried to block it out … her husband actually being shot at….

"You know your father doesn't expect you to follow in his footsteps. He wants you to choose what you want for yourself. We both want you to choose for yourself."

"I know," said Andrew, "I know …" and his voice trailed off.

But he also knew that wasn't really true…. Andrew knew his mom and dad would have strong feelings against his moving forward with what Andrew was considering. Choosing from the heart had downstream complications. Yet none the less the commitment papers for Annapolis lay pristine, without any ink on the page, and the application for STATESIDE's cadet training program was completed. Heart one; head nothing.

"I could be there in less than a week," he told himself, thinking about the STATESIDE option. The training program was only two years … he could defer to Annapolis and learn to pilot in the Cadet training program at STATESIDE; if he liked it great … he could stay, then precept then intern and walk away with a Bachelor's degree; and if not, after two years he would only be twenty ... still eligible even to enter the Academy given his appointment.

'We would both be gone,' Andrew thought, studying his mother for a moment.

He knew she missed his father when he was gone. And sometimes they went weeks at a time without communication, or with limited communication as he was setting up operations in the field, location classified. And then the abrupt calls to move out as missions would pop up suddenly, especially when STATESIDE was short-handed for pilots. Andrew admired his dad for that: for stepping in to fly ground or transport.

"For Heaven's sake, Scott, stay out of harms way," she cautioned him. But Andrew knew his mom also loved the fact that her husband was doing something he believed in, something that helped so many, and something that he loved.

Andrew knew his mom worked hard at keeping him in the know with respect to the spectacular moments of life he missed while in deployment. So she flashed that Polaroid – during Andrew's eighth grade graduation, his cousin's baptism and last Christmas, when they ate alone together. At the dinner table, she said a prayer in thanks, then popped her head up and chided, "How can your father miss these un-missable moments of life, Andrew! You and he should be thankful that I know how to use this!"

And before he knew it he was framed in the lens of the Polaroid, another post to the refrigerator door. Andrew smirked, but he secretly enjoyed the parade of life photos, where he and dad invariably starred as her two leading men.

As he thought about the choices that lay between his head and his heart, he felt conflicted. Annapolis was definitely what his mom wanted. She did not want him to enter STATESIDE's cadet training program. As for his dad, well he said time and again that a military career as an officer has a lot to offer. But in the end, he left one behind to start his own company. And, the conversations between he and his father always concluded with "choose from your heart son. Your heart has reasons that your head won't ever feel."

That just left Andrew with uncertainty. Did he have what it takes to make it through the Academy? How would he know if he was he making the right choice? How much longer did he have before it was too late? Andrew wished his dad were here, as time was running out. It's not like he could really talk to his mother about it. And it's not like he had a lot of friends here. Now if Mr. Sebastian were here, he could talk it out with him. He was someone who he could talk to. Talk open, honestly. He was someone who would listen, and not push his own agenda. Andrew knew he was running out of time. It would soon be time to choose.

Deep down inside, Andrew felt his truth rising up to the surface and that only made things worse.

I did it once and it turned out all right, he thought referring to his choice to leave California.

Amanda finished shaking out a Polaroid photo while watching her son who finally broke free from a lost state of contemplation. Amanda watched Andrew get up, and walk over to the rail.

"Are you going to stay and watch the meet?" She asked her son.

But Andrew offered no response. Andrew was lost again, this time locked in a tight stare, attention focused on a group of swimmers stretching out in front of the starting blocks on the pool deck. Amanda she saw her son studying them, his energy taking on a different hue now, than what she had earlier observed. No, this stare was not a contemplative moment of meditation at all. Amanda saw Andrew zeroed in, and she smiled.

"She's pretty," Amanda admitted to herself.

CHAPTER 10

July 2, 2012
Steward Township Hospital
07:25

"Almost 7:30," Grettie said to Dr. James 'Jon' Mackenzie, Cmdr., US Navy, retired, as she glanced at her watch, waiting in front of the unit clerk's desk.

"Give them a moment Grettie, I'm sure they are full of nervous energy, the first day and all," Dr. Mackenzie replied waiting for the double doors to open.

'He looks sharp,' she thought, as she eyed his pressed white lab coat, name embroidered in bold blue, salt and pepper black hair, cut short.

'I wonder if I will look that young at sixty,' she thought to herself.

"We always leave from medical HQ at 07:30," Grettie heard from somewhere in the pack as the double doors to the ICU opened usurping white coats and scrubs en masse.

"You guys are nervous to present today, aren't you?" she heard Dr. Simi ask the interns on his team during a quick pre-game huddle as the group gathered around the desk just past the magnetic double doors that separated the hallway from the ICU beds.

Grettie recognized all the senior residents, in their green scrubs and mid-length white lab coats. Grettie observed the new crop of young concerned interns, who trailed in short white lab coats without a stain or smudge on them, and she could not help but smile as she picked out the medical students in their very short white lab coats, pockets stuffed with manuals, stethoscope, ophthalmoscope and three pens and a highlighter, their overstuffed pockets making them waddle like baby ducklings walking in single file.

"Are you guys any good at it? Good at presenting?" Dr. Simi asked observing beads of sweat forming on the brow of the interns and other second years residents.

"Presenting is only part of your grade, you know. Now if you are confident, you definitely want them to know who you are," Simi said flipping the picture ID that the interns Dr. Losha and Dr. Davies wore backwards on their lab coats.

"I plan on presenting today," Dr. Simi told the pair,

"so don't sweat it; I've already assessed everyone on Dr. MacKenzie's service; I have all the labs and I've reviewed all the x-rays and reports to give a concise bullet to the senior residents and Attendings on rounds today. Before the day is done, Dr. Mackenzie will know who I am!" Simi said looking down and adjusting his own badge, making sure it was face up.

"You know, it was only one year ago that I stood where you are. And it stinks; one year out of medical school, a licensed physician, yet you are unqualified to do anything on your own. Frustrating right? Have to have a resident or attending's permission to prescribe even an aspirin. Now as a second year resident, I will be allowed to perform some procedures without supervision. Stick close and I may throw you a few procedures like lines or wires," Simi said to the two interns.

"Grettie, how did orientation go? Are the interns and residents getting with the program?" asked Dr. Mackenzie.

"I'll let you know in few minutes," Grettie said, smiling, listening to the second year resident finish torturing the interns.

'Don't worry, you will soon learn how to swim in the real world,' she thought.

From around a corner, Grettie watched the charge nurse appear in royal blue scrubs, no coat, with pens stuck in all four of her cargo pants pockets, black clogs and roll of tape clipped to an oversized safety pin.

In short order the case manager arrived wearing a pretty, colorful skirt. She was followed by the pharmacist and her flock of students all wearing forest green scrubs, pressed and creased neatly. Grettie saw the anticipation and consternation in the eyes of the new second years residents and the fresh interns as they gathered with their assigned teams of nurses and techs.

"Hey Mac," Grettie asked quietly, to her compatriot of twenty years, "how old do you have to be these days to get into medical school?" pointing at a young man smiling in braces!

"Seems to me like they let them in right outta high school with a high school GED," she said.

Dr. Mac smiled, "Yes, maybe time for us to pass on the torch. Retire."

"Retire, yes I see."

But Grettie knew that wasn't about to happen. After Twenty years of teaching, Dr. Mac still looked forward to the new crop of medical students and residents that appeared on the doorstep of Steward Township Hospital every July 1st. Here to learn surgical technique, post op care, and more importantly, here to learn that every kindness counts.

Grettie watched Dr. Mac set up STP with a willingness to take the ordinary and make it special. After his intention was set, the rest just came together like pieces of a puzzle.

"I asked for a chessboard," he said, "And I received Kings and Queens, not to mention a few angels."

Others said he just got lucky. But Grettie knew that's one thing Dr. Mac did not believe in.

"No such thing as luck," he said. "And no one comes into your life randomly."

Grettie knew Dr. Mackenzie was right. Dr. Mac attracted the key people to participate in STP, and luck had nothing to do with it. It was as if they were drawn in like paperclips to a magnet.

In the quiet of his closed office door, he would explain to those with an interest how the co-creative forces of the divine had a hand in actualizing the program.

No, luck had nothing to do with it. Grettie saw it: the right people were pulled in place at the right time as if following some spiritual script.

"People are attracted to integrity, and they will want to be a part of it," he said to her. "They will be pulled forward as if by their own destiny."

"Field of dreams eh?"

"What's that?"

"If you build it they will come!"

"They were already here! Look at Sister Mary Grace!"

The best thing they ever did was convert the East wing to a convent, a hallway walk from their residence to the ICU, she thought. The idea of converting the old adjoining wing of Steward Township Hospital into a convent took some lobbying. But Dr. Mac finessed it with brilliance.

The Sisters provided board for out of town families when needed. And their presence on the wards, and in the rooms added a special standard. The attitudes of the staff, doctors and nurses were markedly respectful around them, as if God's surrogates demanded a higher decorum. Although it might seem strange to some, it really worked. Dr. Mac believed that the harder they worked at technique and patient care and sticking to the founding principles of compassionate care without judgments, the better they became, the better were the outcomes. Grettie watched Dr. Mac operate in the OR by night, and by his principles during the day. She heard him tell the residents, "we will never really know why those that come to us do so; but treat it as if each patient is here by appointment ... why not; what have you got to lose?" he asked.

"Be on the look out for it; because good things happen in the presence of kindness and compassion. So don't judge them; just try to help in the ways we know how to help. That is how every kindness counts, you see."

And, after all, it worked for her, Grettie thought. Although Grettie was there before Dr. Mackenzie ever came to Steward Township Hospital, she was eager to sign up and work with him when the Trauma Nurse Manager position was posted. Grettie had been an experienced nurse administrator who had an interest in holism yet no where to really dig into it; she was happy to come join Dr. Mackenzie all those years ago and use her caring skills along with the organizational aspects of the program. She was proud to be one of those key people, and it showed; in her enthusiasm, in her attitude, in her dress and attention toward being the compassionate caring health care professional that STP strived to create.

Although skeptical at first, Grettie came to understand how kindness seemed to be an important catalyst-like cream into grits – supporting the very substance of what went into recovery. The medical team would do the surgery; they would meet to study and discuss theory, the science of new medicines, new techniques and provide dressings and fluids and antibiotics; and then, when the science was in the patient's system, the medical team would stand back and watch destiny play out. Dr. Mac said it over and over again. Injury and illness is a spiritual event. And that is why he valued Sister

Mary Grace and her special blend of insight, caring and wisdom to all his cases: she would sit and pray with the patients, meet with the families, often somehow turning doom and gloom into laughter and celebration and support the very fabric of all that was really important in life. "Let go and let God," she would say.

And besides, even if it wasn't true, even if it had no medical power, it couldn't hurt. What was to be lost by spending a little time in prayer? And who was to discount the power of prayer in the recovery of the injured and ill? Grettie knew that Dr. Mac believed it was one of those things that science couldn't tackle and logic couldn't explain. Prayer seemed to be one of those mysteries: an abstract concept, but with concrete effects. Grettie knew that Dr. Mac was careful to separate principles that were spiritual, from religion, as many faiths entered those doors. He did not try to force any specific belief on any of the patrons or staff of Steward.

Through the years, she and Dr. Mac, with the help of interested residents had published a few articles on the program ... but it is difficult to study the power of kindness academically. And that's what science wanted: academic, peer reviewed reproducible data on outcomes. And Dr. Mac knew that would never happen. He could not study it, he could not measure it, he could not operate on it, but one thing he did know was that a soul was involved in every fall, fail and trauma; and what was more, was that unpredictability was the rule. Soul work: a mystery between science and spirit, and it was all around him in the walls and halls of Steward Township Hospital. That is why Grettie knew he would never leave. It was as if he had stumbled on the soul work of his own life.

At this point in his career, Grettie understood that stewardship had eclipsed surgical technique and science. His position as program chair was an opportunity for him to guide the young physicians who survived med school and residency and offer a glimpse at higher consciousness. He understood, he knew, that he could most positively influence his team by modeling what he preached. Punctual, pressed white coat with shirt and tie when not in the OR; and respectful to all who gathered with him, considerate of their time and effort. He was an attentive listener – and he often stopped the younger residents and taught a session on what it was to be an active listener.

For Grettie, Dr. Mac's approach was a model of compassionate care. For over twenty years, she watched him evolve to the point where he served the patients who came through those doors. She knew that he believed that the patients themselves gave him an opportunity to be a healthcare professional. His job was to help in the ways possible, and to do no harm. She knew that there was one unyielding principle that he espoused throughout his career: regardless of how or why anyone became injured or ill, each life was deserving of equal respect; he called it the sanctity of life; and being entrusted with a life was not only a great responsibility, but a great gift given to them all. A gift not to be taken lightly.

She knew that Military life had laid the groundwork of his foundation. They spent time talking about how the soldier and the resident went through a similar evolution, and they both knew that it was easy for the residents to lose themselves like many soldiers had, as they became bombarded, day after day with incoming nameless faces, burns and falls and gunshot wounds and stabbings; blunt abdominal trauma and head injuries and broken bones; trauma was bloody, urgent and – sometimes senseless – just like battle. Entering through the ER doors, some presented with self-inflicted wounds, some presented with wounds inflicted by others: gangs and knives and guns, and cars and assaults. The circumstance in battle might have been different, but the injuries the street offered were the same: and the pace of urgency in each, exhausting. By the second or third month on the trauma service, many of Dr. Mac's residents would be in danger of becoming jaded. He knew first hand how easy it would be to become jaded over times. Toiling in blood, and violence, picking up the pieces of gang wars and stabbings was at times confusing to the residents and the other Attendings. He knew the frustrating futility of their efforts first hand and he was careful to spot the drop into resentful scorn that could spread like wildfire. For that was human nature ... fatigued tired at 02:30 when an ambulance drops of a wounded civilian with multiple gun shot wounds the police state were 'gang related' ... it was natural to condemn the insanity of it all.

Grettie was not sure what sparked Dr. Mac's evolution. She did not know exactly when he began to realize the sanctity of life in the muck of the city streets that joined to counties; but somehow he became interested in compassionate care without judgment; maybe it was time, maybe it was despair, and maybe it was the deep surrender into his search for meaning in all the killing and murder of life. But somewhere along the line his soul had awakened, his awareness deepened and he saw life beyond circumstance. He saw opportunity for spiritual retribution, and the gathering of grace in acts of heroism. He recognized each trauma victim as a soul in some state of reckoning. Maybe, just maybe they could be led up from a bottom that would springboard them into a deeper awareness, and they too might see with new eyes, like he had seen. How life and death are inter-

connected at the doorway of the ER. And how intercon-
nected we all are by the similarity of our own existence.

At this point in his career, the ER doors were as
sacred as the cathedral doors to a church; sinners and
saints alike entered, each disguised, broken and bloody-
each 'working out their karma' she would hear him say.
There was one thing that Grettie was sure of: Dr. Mac
believed that each body that rolled in to the door of the
ER was no lesser or greater than any other. To each he
gave the respect he believed they deserved by virtue of
the divinity of their existence. "Get them fixed as best as
you can," he would tell the residents, "that's your job. By
doing your best regardless of the guns and knives and
gangs, you bring grace into this world," he told them.
"There is honor in the effort. And honor yields integrity."

"Life is sacred...and to teach that principle year in
and year out is an honor," he said. Grettie watched that
principle slowly sink in to the residents rotating through
Steward Township Hospital. In the end, it was one of
the things Dr. Mac was most respected for. Teaching the
principles of STP while he worked at living it.

"STP ... compassion without judgment: you all will
at least be exposed to it this year. Whether you learn it
or not is up to you."

Grettie saw Dr. Mac move his eyes past the young
residents in lab coats, past the social services team and

their pretty summer dresses, to ICU-1 where he caught a glimpse of Sister Mary Grace through the reflection of the mirror in ICU-1, and she saw him smile.

"STP at its finest," he whispered to Grettie, as the throng of many voices huddled around ICU bed -1.

Chapter 11

TV 14406 heard a throng of voices as if coming from the pool deck; too many voices and too far away for him to make out anything more than sounds. Andrew realized the team was huddled at the pool deck, and even though he knew he shouldn't, he kept a lock on her. He watched her move with ease, and grace through the gathering of swimmers. Pretty, mesmerizing, she captured his full attention.

———

August 27, 2004

Meza Sports Complex
Stadium Seats

10 AM

Andrew watched Beth pull her hair out of the racing cap, and then pull off the goggles covering her chocolate brown eyes. And although he tried not to stare, he could not help himself. He quickly became lost in her form. He watched her walk up to her boyfriend as Pat called the team together. She was tall, about five foot nine he guessed, Chestnut hair, long and flowing. He watched her pull her swim cap off and he thought back to yesterday, when he stood close enough to her to breathe in the vanilla that floated up in wafts of flavor from her shiny hair. Still captivated by the smile and the look behind eyes that just drew him in during their encounter yesterday, Andrew couldn't help wonder what it would be like to be with her.

But she belonged to Pat; and he seemed all right, Andrew admitted. And they are probably King and Queen of the Prom, Andrew thought.

Amanda Galloway could not help noticing, as mother's do, her son's fixed attention on a pretty auburn-haired, long legged girl, down on the pool deck. Amanda smiled recognizing the spark.

When Andrew looked up again, his heart jumped. Pat was pointing up at him from the center of the huddle and the whole team was fixated on him. Andrew lifted his head completely upright.

'Great,' he thought, 'what in the world could this be about?'

———

August 27, 2004

Meza Sports Complex
Pool Deck

10 AM

"Big meet today," Pat said as he gathered the team around him, standing in the center of the huddle.

"The lane assignments are posted, so everyone check your heet sheets before we get started. Good luck," he went on encouragingly. "One change today, though, in the final open 4x100 meter relay ..." Pat's tonality shifted to concern.

"Ozzie and Bird are not going to make it." The Highway is closed and traffic is backed up for hours coming in from the west side. It would take a helicopter to get them here on time. And to win the team championship, we need to win the relay. It would be nice to hang a banner in the field house with all our names on the wall of honor," he pointed to the stadium.

Ozzie had been great off the block. Bird a solid second leg, followed by Caz and then Pat at anchor: a combination that had won every 4x100 open relay that they had swam together.

"Oh, Pat, man ... No Ozzie and Bird!" Caz emoted.

"I know … it hurts, but I think I know of a way we can still win this … but it will require an open mind."

Caz looked with disgust at the underclassman.

"Pattie if there is a way to win, then we need to try it. This is the last one for you and me. We owe it to ourselves to try and hang a banner on the wall. But unless you got a pocket superman, it's not going to happen," replied Caz. "No one has enough speed to make up for Oz and Birdman."

"Caz is right … I'll need a junior to step up here."

"Lot's of tradition here: Power Pride baby," Caz said as he looked around the group of underclassmen. "DJ" … Caz added, "you are probably the next fastest – get pumped … and Jenkins, today is your day, a sophomore man, swimming with the seniors today … can you go a personal best for the team?"

Pat looked at DJ and Jenkins, and smiled.

"Even if DJ breaks his personal best, fifty-seven seconds for a hundred, is not going to get it done today," Pat said.

"Well they are the two fastest guys we got Pat. It's got to be one of these two guys, no?"

"No, Caz … not exactly."

"Beth," Pat called out.

Pat found Beth in the outer edge of the assembled group breaking her attention as she had her head turned, as if off into the crowd. "You're in. You go off the blocks first."

Caz looked up at Pat as if to say, 'are you kidding me?' But Pat averted the backlash.

"It's an open relay, and you are just as fast as DJ and Jenkins. Need you in around 57 Beth, so swim hard," he said.

"OK, then DJ goes the second leg ... Caz added trying to be helpful ... right?"

"No, not DJ Caz."

"Then who bra?"

"You Caz ... you swim second."

"Me? What? You and me, Bra, third and anchor, as always."

"Not today Caz ... keep an open mind."

"You are going to put DJ third instead of me? What kind of strategy is that, Pat man?" asked Caz feeling slighted.

"No, DJ is not going to swim third instead of you, Caz."

"Well who is third then?"

"I am," Pat replied. "I will be right behind you as always, Caz. You got my front; I got your back. You follow my sister, and I follow you. We can do this."

"Oh Pattie," Caz said, "Then what? DJ anchors the relay? Why? It makes no sense Pat!"

"No … DJ you are going to have to sit this one out. You and Jenkins will have your moment, but not today."

"Then who is going to swim anchor?" Caz asked in full emotional charge.

"With any kind of luck, he will …" and Pat pointed up into the stands, at the sandy-brown haired, green-eyed muscular teenager who was staring right dead center into their huddle, from the bottom row of the bleachers.

In an instant, all eyes fell upon Andrew.

"What!! … Pat you've lost it. That guy you were talking to yesterday? You don't even know him. And come on Pat, he's not one of us."

"No Caz, he is one of us. He is a new one of us. He lives in the school district, close to you, and will be starting classes here next week, just like you and I. He is new to town, and part of this community now, and we need to all welcome him."

"And Caz," Pat added, "he's fast. I got him yesterday at fifty-three for a hundred. Fifty-three Caz! We need him," Pat added. "So you're going to just go up and invite to come swim with us …?" Caz asked with disgust.

"No," Pat said. "*Beth* and I are going to go up there and get him. I invited him yesterday to swim with us in workout, but he did not want to. But he was sure interested in you Beth…." Pat looked over at his sister, hoping she would play along.

"Oh so now you are pimping out your sister to get this guy to swim? Come on Pat, it's time for DJ or Sloop or Jenkins or one of the other juniors to step up and lead off; we'll be just fine. We can catch anyone, Pat, you and me," he said with hubris, his bravado getting the better of him.

"That's fine, Pat," Beth said. "I'll go talk to him. Besides, he's kind of cute ..." Beth said glancing past Caz's rant, sensing her brother's need for help.

"Whatever man, you are the captain, do what you what feel," replied Caz hands on his hips in disgust.

———

Meza Athletic Complex
Stadium Seats
10:20

Amanda spot-checked her son while walking and talking to coaches and reporters needing heat sheets Internet access and printers. The Kraft service contractors had food and juice and coffee set up in the tent next to the bleachers near to where Andrew sat. Amanda felt her son's pulse quicken, and she saw his eyes get big as a handsome young man about his age with wet hair wearing gym shorts and a tee shirt approached along with the pretty young girl who held her son's attention earlier.

"I can see why he likes her," Amanda Galloway said to herself, as she scanned the silhouette of the auburn haired girl. Her racing suit was clinging tightly to her shapely top, with tight fitting gym shorts below, waistband rolled down below her hips.

Amanda saw Andrew go from sitting head down elbow on knees, to head up hands on knees, to head up, sitting straight up, hands on thighs.

———

'Oh no … what's this about?' Andrew breathed to himself feeling himself back on guard.

Andrew watched Pat and his girlfriend approach. Andrew mentally played a hundred scenarios over in his mind. If he had to, Andrew was ready to apologize. He didn't mean to stare impolitely, he couldn't help himself.

'Oh great,' he said to himself, 'not only am I going to apologize, but also I'm going to do this in front of my mother! How humiliating!'

Andrew stood up and considered an escape route out through the media tent.

"No," he said, "I've got to get this over with … let's take this one straight on."

Andrew guessed Pat was an inch or two shorter than he was, maybe six one, but Pat was muscular and lean. He was a good swimmer though... clean, and efficient in the water. And in warm-ups, Beth looked nearly as good as he was. She was the only girl in the fast lane with the senior boys and she seemed to hold her own. And out of the water, she was amazing. Her curvy legs and strong haunches were both athletic and sexy, and he became embarrassed as he thought it. After all, that's what landed him in this trouble in the first place. As her hair bounced and flowed loosely, still wet, he noticed her brown eyes locked on him, and his body responded to a mind perceiving trouble. Andrew's pulse quickened, and he felt sweat on his brow like he was beginning a 220 yard sprint around the track.

"Hi Andrew," began Beth.

Andrew stood immediately, his face whitening. "Glad you came by today," Beth went on with Pat standing silently beside her.

"Hello," Andrew said surprisedly, glancing back and forth waiting for Pat to engage him. Andrew focused his attention on Pat, trying to get a read on him, but his attention was quickly called back to the playful, fun eyes of Beth. His inner dialogue consumed his mind and he was lost in her. Her lips were full and round, and he watched her mouth move. Her long hair was wet, but pulled free from her cap, up in a bun, showing off a single spiral earring that glistened in the summer sun. Andrew could smell the scent of Vanilla, as her hair emanated flavor in wafts again, just like yesterday.

"My brother and I were wondering ..." Beth thumbed

over to Pat, "well, hoping really," she went on, her tone softening, and her body language adopting the posture of a woman in need, "that...."

Andrew knew Beth was still talking, but his inner world stopped processing information after he heard the words 'my brother.'

Brother? Did she say brother?

Andrew blocked out the content of the sentences that followed. He watched Beth moving her mouth, and he knew words were being spoken, but that was her brother, not her boyfriend. Andrew perceived the muffled sounds of Beth's voice and her brown eyes held him captive while his thought within his own mind ricocheted off in a tangent. He looked past her eyes as she went on, her words skipping over his awareness like a stone across a lake. He took in her radiance, but did not hear sound, his attention focused inward processing his own all-consuming inner dialog. Awake, but lost in the moment, he began to process the implications of what he had just heard.

Huh, her brother, not her boyfriend ... that's interesting ... he thought. Makes sense though. They rode together every morning he had seen them training at the sports complex. The two always came and left together, in the orange jeep. He had just assumed he picked her up and brought her to workout. No wonder he wasn't ticked at me when I was staring at her right in front of him, Andrew thought. Makes perfect sense, he thought, her brother, not her boyfriend. Then I wonder whose girlfriend she is? Maybe … no, not that Caz character … although I bet he would want her to be … but she's to cool for him … maybe no-one? Humph, what are the odds of that? Maybe, just maybe I have a chance with her.

Andrew dialed back in to the moment, breaking free from captivity. He could not hold back the beginnings of a smile as he was released from her brown eyes, and he watched her red lips moving, catching up to the meaning behind her words.

"So, do you think you could help us out?" he heard her ask him.

"Oh, sure I can help," Andrew responded automatically. "Happy to help."

"Great said Pat! Go get your gear!"

"Wait, what?"

Andrew darted between Beth and Pat, confusion written all over his face.

"I'm sorry … what do you want me to do?" Andrew asked Beth, fully present now, no daydreams, no internal dialogue, just a quickening pulse and his own flushed face.

"Just that one race, that's all we need," Pat answered,

"you'll have plenty of time to get signed in and get registered. All you need is your driver's license. Go around into the tent, register, and they'll give you a swimmer's pass to get downstairs. If you hustle you can get a quick warm up in the diving pool, then I'll introduce you to the team," Pat said enthusiastically and he broke away hustling back toward his teammates.

"Wait...." Andrew reached out and lightly clasped Beth's wrist as she began to follow her brother. "What am I doing?" he asked embarrassedly, his fluster wearing off. Beth looked into Andrew's green eyes and softly smiled.

"You didn't hear anything I said, did you...."

"Well, I sort of got some of the beginning, about him being your brother... and, well it's just that I was well ... and then I got some of the end, but mostly the very end of it ... the part about help. And you know I'm real good around the pool, timer, heats, lane ropes ...you know."

Beth held his gaze, warmly, with light hearted empathy, and crossed her arms across her chest, stepping back shifting her weight onto her back leg, enjoying the flustering stumbling as the man-boy in front of her went on. She couldn't help but enjoy how those big green eyes of her fish on the line dilated big and then searched her face. He was cute, she thought, and she enjoyed the feeling knowing he was hooked.

"I mean I could be a timer for your club, and I

could stay and take the chairs down afterwards, clear off the pool deck, pull the lane ropes, if that's what you need," said Andrew trying to recover. Andrew's eyes had emerged from space and were almost pleading with her to undo what he had done.

Beth softened, amused by this big handsome stranger all flustered and embarrassed. She tilted her head slightly to one side and stared deeply into big green eyes, holding his gaze, and thought him a bit endearing. Skittish as a little kitty, but big and strong, definitely masculine, she thought: but somehow not like the other guys around here. She couldn't help feel that he was sincere. Somewhere in those emerald green eyes, she got the feeling that he was for real. Beth processed the feeling, and she liked it. While most of these other boys would jump at the opportunity to impress her, here was this new guy ... a perfect stranger ... clearly interested, but yet somehow polite, respectful and different.

"You're cute," she said, smiling, face to face, and she turned her palm upwards taking his hand in hers, "agreeing to *help out* and all ... But right now you are going to race with us, OK? We need you to swim, just like you did yesterday, just like you have been doing almost every morning this week, OK?" She took both hands, dipped her head, and looked at him squarely, trying to be sure he was programmed.

"The relay is the last event of the meet, so maybe after you swim with us, you can stay and put away the lane ropes, and help out the maintenance crew," Beth laughed a bit... Cute or not, she was having too much fun to let this fish off the hook.

"You should go change and get a warm-up swim in. The relay should go off in a little while. See you on deck," she said going on as if she were instructing a grade-schooler.

Andrew blushed full on now, releasing Beth's hand, as she began to walk away, embarrassed by his stupidity. After five feet, she looked back, and said playfully, "By the way, my name is Beth, just in case you did not catch it yesterday."

Andrew nodded his head and partially rolled his eyes as she smiled back at him as she walked away.

"Like I could forget that," he said not loudly enough for her to hear.

Andrew watched Beth walk away, tan, tall, fit and so sexy.

"How about that," he said to himself ... "His sister."

Andrew watched until she became lost in the pack. "Jeez," Andrew said realizing the moment, "I might be done with racing, but it seems that racing isn't done with me...."

Chapter 12

Monday, July 2, 2012
Steward Township Hospital
07:30 AM

"Well, good morning everyone," Dr. Mackenzie said, salt and pepper grey hair spiked up in a military style crew cut, wearing a white lab coat pressed and starched, over a white shirt and a tie, as the team quieted in front of the doorway to ICU bed-1.

"It's been a while since resident interviews and I want to know each one of you by name. So please wear you name badges facing outward so all the staff can see them," he said flipping his name badge right side over so his picture and name were clearly visible under the embroidered lapel over his front pocket.

"As you may or may not know, at a teaching hospital such as this one, the patients are assigned to attending physicians like myself, Dr. Childs and Dr. Montgomery.

You will be rotating with each attending every three months or so. I make rounds each morning at 07:30, and I will ask the assigned residents to present the patients as we go. See one, do one, teach one, you know. So let's just jump right in, shall we Dr. Williams?"

The nurse handed the vitals sheet over to Dr. Mackenzie who open-endedly asked, "OK, who can present this patient?"

Williams nodded to Simi, and Simi squeezed to the center to face Dr. Mackenzie.

"ICU bed 1, TV 14406, a no information patient, male, who appears to be involved in a motorcycle accident —while trying to fly," Dr. Simi said with a chuckle, "as he arrived wearing a parachute. He suffered a head injury with facial and pharyngeal swelling, some bleeding, and looks like inhalation burns," he began the bullet summary describing the patient's condition in medical parlance.

"He contused his cervical cord but his spine is stable, no surgery planned, and there's no intracranial bleeding. Neurosurgery recommended Decadron for the spinal cord and brain swelling and signed off; so for now he is a breather and feeder," finished Simi.

"Thank you, eh…." Dr. Mac leaned in to catch the name on Simi's credential badge, "Dr. Simi," he paused. "Well medically presented."

"Any Social history?"

"Details are sketchy sir; but surprisingly, the tox screen that Dr. Childs ordered was negative; no amphetamines or hallucinogenics," Simi went on.

"I see," said Dr. Mackenzie. "Why is that surprising."

"Well at St. Stephens, where I trained, most of these high speed risk takers were either jacked up on coke or tripping on LSD."

"And is that the case with this young man?" Dr. Mackenzie asked.

"Although that is likely, we don't know much about this case, sir."

"Why is that Dr. Simi?"

"Well sir, there are a few cryptic notes in the chart, but no details."

"So your presumption is based on other 'cases' you have attended to in the past?"

"Yes, sir. At St. Stephens most of these types of cases involved players loaded on crystal meth, cheese, or – burning rubber on a crotch rocket."

"These 'players in these types of cases', yes, I see," said Dr. Mackenzie. "Well do the best you can for him, Dr. Simi; let's try to reserve judgment. With our limited perspective we can't always see the whole picture."

"So, what is your plan for this patient, Dr. Simi?"

"Well, he looks pretty stable, and I think we can begin reversing him," Dr. Simi glanced up to receive a confirming nod from Dr. Williams, "and see if we can get him off the vent; if he fails, we are looking at a trach and PEG; it will be easier to feed him and breathe him."

"Feed him and breathe him, yes I see."

"Yes sir," Simi said "and I've got experience placing them both, sir, if you need a second scrub," Simi finished as Williams just stared down at the floor with his hand over his forehead.

"Yes, I see," Dr. Mackenzie acknowledged. "Thank you, I will take that in the spirit it was offered as an opportunity to be of service."

Dr. Mackenzie turned to the group and said, "OK, let's be sure the medical students and the interns understand what we are referring to here. Dr. Williams, do you mind explaining."

"No problem Dr. Mackenzie," Williams replied and he turned to face the group.

"Right now, the patient is on a ventilator sending air into his lungs through a tube; an endotracheal tube. His body is getting needed oxygen and based on his blood oxygen levels that we monitor on the screen, oxygen delivery is OK. The endotracheal tube can be fragile; patients can pull it out fairly easily and so we generally keep them sedated; converting the endotracheal tube into a tracheostomy will allow for better airway control and better oxygen delivery; and although it is a surgery, we can do that at bedside here in the ICU. So reversing him means stopping sedation and allowing him to regain consciousness. We would do that when we think his lungs are improved enough that he will be able to breathe on his own.

As far as nutrition goes, he is getting some hydration by IV fluids, but the fluids short him calories and nutrients. By dropping a feeding tube down, we can support his nutritional needs. It is a more permanent mechanism to provide nutrition, used when we think recovery is going to be a bit protracted. We can do that procedure in interventional radiology."

"Thank you Dr. Williams," Dr. Mackenzie said. "So, back to the rubber meeting the road … what's next?"

"Well I am still waiting for the police rundown."

"A police rundown? What made you think of that?"

"We did that fairly routinely at St. Stephens. Often, the no information patients had been through the system once or twice before. So I wouldn't be surprised if this isn't this guy's first trip through the system. These types of cases usually end up in jail. And that's how it should be; we need to get these guys off the streets. They might kill someone flying out of control all jacked up like that."

"Well next time, why don't we wait on notifying the police until we have some details of the occurrence. In my experience, Dr. Simi the details usually come to light just as they are supposed to."

"Let's get social service involved on this one, shall we? Who has got him?" Dr. Mackenzie scanned the group.

"That would be me," said a voice in the crowd.

"Ah, hello Jill," said Dr. Mac looking over to the social worker. "Will you see what you can do for us on this one? See if we can find out who he is, and a few details of what happened? That might help deepen all of our perspectives," Dr. Mac finished.

"Absolutely sir, it would be my pleasure!"

The team turned and smiled at the enthusiasm with which Jill answered. Not facetious, but well rehearsed maybe. Dr. Mac gave Jill a knowing wink, and said, "not your first rodeo, eh?"

"No sir, Dr. Mackenzie," replied the social worker.

"OK, any other thoughts?" Dr. Mackenzie asked turning to the team.

"Yes that you should move on to ICU-2" came the reply from Grettie.

After a group laugh, Dr. Mackenzie bowed in deference, "Yes, I suppose we should," he said.

Williams knew that only Grettie could get away with that.

Dr. Mac moved to walk off to the next patient, but abruptly stopped outside the door of the room, with Simi almost walking into him from behind.

"Dr. Simi," he asked, "if Jill tracks down this boy's identity and by chance happens to see this patient's mother, what should she tell her?"

"What?"

"If Jill, here, were this patient's mother, what would you tell her?"

"I'm sorry sir?"

"Go ahead, talk to her. Talk to Jill as if she was the boy's mother. If you had to explain the situation, what would you tell her?" Dr. Mac went on.

"Well, I'd probably, well not probably, but maybe ..." and Simi looked at Jill who couldn't help but smile at the uncomfortable second year caught off guard by the role playing, "given that all the consults are completed and such that the CT was really unimpressive, and labs look OK, and with the facial edema and all, I would probably tell her that...."

"Ahhh, you loved her from the moment you saw her, didn't you my son," came the voice from the concealed bedside chair back within the room.

The group laughed en masse again, as from within the room, Sister Mary Grace's timing provided impeccable comic relief.

Dr. Mac looked back in through the open door, craning his neck around the corner and smiled.

"That's Sister Mary Grace from Grace of Souls, sir,"

offered Simi, as if Dr. Mac was unaware of whom she was.

"Good Morning Sister Mary Grace from Grace of Souls" Dr. Mac replied rat-a-tat-tat.

In short order, Simi began presenting the nun to Dr. Mac and the group as if she was a patient.

"Sister Mary Grace comes every day to sit with the trauma patients, console their families and pray. She doesn't see well, doesn't hear well, she might even have a touch of dementia."

With that last comment, Dr. Mac pulled back from the room.

"Why do you say that?" Dr. Simi.

"Well, I was here earlier sir, on pre-rounds, and I heard her talking to herself."

"And you think she has dementia because talks to herself?" Dr. Mac stopped now addressing the group as they formed a trail behind him stopping in front of ICU-2.

"Yes sir, I'd say she likely has some Age Related Cognitive Decline or Alzheimer's Dementia. Now Age Related Macular degeneration is the most likely cause of failing vision in patients her age, effecting vision, I mean, and Alzheimer's Dementia, sir, being the most common cause of memory loss in a person of her age range ... and that would be my guess, sir." Simi offered the diagnoses.

"Talks to herself and does not see ..." Dr. Mac mused, "How interesting."

"Well, Dr. Simi, 'seeing' is an interesting paradox. When you looked over this young man this morning, what did you see?"

"I saw a twenty some-thingish male, 3 days post injury, vented and sedated with facial and pharyngeal edema. I also saw his tests; a brain CT without bleeding or contusions. I saw his labs – electrolyte panel and CBC looked OK. I saw the consult reports from neurology and neurosurgery and I saw the internal medicine intern's note – Good report by the way Losha – I saw it all sir. I don't think I missed anything sir," Dr. Simi concluded.

"So basically, Dr. Simi, this morning, you saw a 23 year old trauma victim unconscious on the vent, asleep," Dr. Mac summarized.

"Yes, sir."

"OK, hold that thought."

Dr. Mackenzie turned his attention back to the bedside chair within ICU-1.

"Sister Mary Grace, good morning."

"Good morning Doctor Mackenzie, so good to see you this morning," she said turning to the sound of his voice.

"Would you mind telling us what you saw when you walked into the room this morning?"

"Certainly. I saw a sacred soul, on a special journey. I saw a soul evolving through the experiences of his life. I saw a young man asleep after colliding with the unexpected, arriving here, where destiny placed him in our care."

"Thank you Sister," said Dr. Mac, "beautifully said from a refreshing perspective.... Thank you for your work with him, and thank you for all the work you are doing here."

"No, thank you, doctor. After all, God works through the people in the world ... and the soul work of life never goes for naught."

"Thank you, Sister."

Dr. Mackenzie led the group outside the room and said, "Who is to say the Sister is wrong? Is it possible, as spiritual beings, that we are each on some wrung of a ladder 'evolving experientially' ... as the good sister said ... in a process that is never ending?"

"Never ending just like our rounds if we don't speed up," blurted out Grettie.

Dr. Mac had a good laugh with the group and was happy to proceed down to ICU-6, the next stop on their rounds.

As the team moved down the hallway, a song followed behind them from within the room of the unknown patient.

"She's singing to him now," Dr. Simi said fighting back a laugh.

"Make me a channel of your peace ..." the song began from within the room of he unknown patient.

"It's The Song of St. Francis, Dr. Simi." Dr. Mac placed his arm around the shoulder of the second year resident and said, "and the intention underlying the song holds great power. You should listen to it some time."

"Yes, sir."

"And one more thing, if by chance today, Dr. Simi, we identify our unknown patient, and you have an opportunity to meet his family, spend a moment to get to know what he was like. Understanding him may change your opinions. We may never know the reason why he is here, but every kindness counts". "Yes sir, got it," Simi said as he put two fingers on his forehead. "Prayer of St. Francis, learn it; every kindness counts."

Simi dropped to the back of the pack and stood behind Williams, out of Dr. Mac's earshot. He shot his senior resident a quick glance and then rolled his eyes and began whispering the tune to 'The Twilight Zone'.

TV 14406 heard the intercom sound, and he realized it was the walkie-talkie that his mother carried at the stadium. "Excuse me ma'am he said, to her. I need a competitor's badge. They need me to swim," he said into the unforgiving ET tube as Dr. MacKenzie's team completed their rounds.

CHAPTER 13

August 27, 2004

Meza Sports Complex

11AM

"Excuse me ma'am," Andrew said walking up to a lady with a walkie-talkie in her hand, "Where can I get a competitor's badge?"

Andrew's mother chuckled. "Very funny son," she said pausing briefly, then going back to her train of thought processing her responsibilities for the swim meet.

"No really, Mom, I've get to get down to the locker room."

"Really?" she said, pausing, looking hard at her son, back pack across his shoulder. "You want to swim?" Amanda Galloway quickly completed her reading of her son's sincere demeanor. 'He's not joking!' she thought.

"Yes, she ... they need me to swim."

"Who wants you to swim, Andrew?"

"The club team, from the high school here."

"The club team … I see," Amanda said, glancing down to the girl who had her eyes fixated on her son.

"Dad and I saw the club team training here ever since we arrived in Meza. We were leaving just as they were arriving here to train. But I met them the other day, and they are short in the relay. So I told them I would help them out, that's all."

"Are you sure you want to do this?" Amanda asked her son.

"Well I already told them I would. Too late to back out now, you know. It's no big deal, it's only a relay. But I need to sign in and register. Name, address, school district … you know the usual. Oh, and I need a badge to get downstairs to change."

"Well I can help you with that … come with me." Amanda walked her son into the media tent.

"Sit here, and smile!" A flash erupted quickly followed by winding gears, and a few moments later a photo was chopped and cropped and laminated. Out came Andrew's mom with a purple laminated card that said 'Athlete.' Amanda placed the badge around his neck. Then quickly, from behind her back, she wielded the Polaroid again, and caught Andrew, straight on with his credentials around his neck.

"So handsome," she smiled, proud of her work. "Your father would be so proud, dear," she said as Andrew rolled his eyes and headed off.

———

11:30 AM

In the space of three longs strides toward the warm up pool, Andrew lost his smile. 'He's smart,' Andrew thought watching Pat with the team. 'He knew I wouldn't say no to her ... after all, she is amazing,' he thought playing the scene over again. 'My Name is Beth, just in case you didn't catch it before ... Hello Beth.... If I mess up, she might never talk to me again,' he thought. 'It's only the one relay ... how bad can that be; and besides, no one here knows me; or will even care ... unless I mess up,' he thought looking at the team gathering poolside.

Andrew stood at the edge of the pool and pulled his goggles over his head. His hands were trembling. Andrew dove into the water for his warm up; he glided easily, breathing every third stroke, alternating breaths; first right then left.

'What have I gotten myself into,' he thought as he approached the wall. 'I really don't want to be here,' and he flipped at the turn missing the wall completely.

"Ah, Pattie, your boy over there, in warm-ups ... just missed the wall ... in warm-ups Pat!"

Floundering near the wall in an awkward and effortful dolphin kick, Andrew tried to ease off into another lap. 'Just great,' he thought as he glided slowly. 'I haven't missed a wall since I was twelve.' Arms heavy with fatigue he remembered that race flipping over and kicking in panic finding only open water. With the terror of the memory fresh, he began breathing every other stroke instead of every fourth.

'I better just get out,' he thought. 'I feel flat as it is.'

Andrew hit the wall and pressed himself up and out of the water when his foot caught the edge; rubber legged and quivering, he fell backward in an awkward splash.

'Thank God no one is watching me,' he thought when he heard Caz call over to him.

"Use the rail rook, don't get hurt before the big race!"

Back down in the warm up pool, his face red, and with perspiration on his brow, Andrew quickly struggled up again, successfully pressing himself up and out.

'I didn't just do that!' Andrew thought scrambling for his towel on rubbery legs, feeling more than one pair of eyes watching him.

"There goes your ace, Pat … can't even make it out of warm-ups," Caz said to his silent captain.

'Stay cool,' Andrew tried to program himself, trying not to become undone under the weight of Caz's glare.

With each step toward the outer circle of the huddled group Andrew felt as if his thigh was about to cramp. He felt as if strength was draining from his body like an open can of coke turned upside down.

'Great, just great' … Andrew thought. 'Really? I thought I was past all this.'

Andrew stood outside the circle of teammates, toweling off the drops of perspiration that had replaced the droplets of chlorinated water from his warm-up. Hands on his knees, head down, he tried to compose himself while peering through the twenty-five pairs of shaven legs of the Meza swim club.

'No surprise here,' he thought noticing that Caz and the other seniors packed together in the first layer of the inside circle with the juniors behind them and the freshman and sophomores one layer removed outside the nucleus of the important players.

'High school culture,' Andrew thought. Grade conferred rank and status.

"OK guys, listen up," Andrew heard Pat from the center.

'Naturally, the captain,' Andrew thought taking in the cool-headed calm. 'I bet he's the Quarterback of the football team, and prom king.'

"OK guys; as expected, it's going to come down to the Four Hundred Free Relay for a banner up there and

a poster in the gym with our names on it," he said pointing past the enormous scoreboard, where the 'Wall of
Honor' streamed banners from the Fieldhouse entrance
like ribbons.

Friday Night Lights, Andrew breathed to himself,
as he looked up to the proud display of a town proud of
its sports legacy. His heart rate began to ramp up just a
little bit.

"Beth, you are off the blocks first."

"Excuse me," Andrew heard her say, and Andrew's
heart rate ticked up as he watched her gather her loose
long brown hair. Beth then ducked her sculpted shoulders on angle slicing through the crowd of her teammates on strong, long tan legs that Andrew thought
were as close to perfect as could be. Wafts of Vanilla
floated back to the outer edge of the circle as Andrew
stood up to track her.

Captivated by her soft voice, fragrant hair, and her
beautiful feminine figure, Andrew's mind etched an un-
forgettable memory in his heart. And his heart rate responded in the only way it could.

'120,' he thought, using his two fingers to measure
his own racing pulse.

With his head up and eyes toward the stone deck
of the Olympic style venue, Andrew tried to pay atten-

tion to Pat, but all he could really pay attention to was a spiral earring shimmering in the summer sun. Andrew fixed his gaze on the vortex of light that was Beth, as she stood shoulder to shoulder with her brother, facing Andrew. Beth's auburn brown hair was tucked up into her white swim-cap that said 'Meza' in bold.

'She is amazing!' he thought.

"We could use a personal best today," Andrew heard Pat say, "so swim hard Beth." Andrew saw Pat wink and smile, pointing behind him up to the scoreboard that would mark Beth's time. "Need you in under a minute Beth."

Andrew, too, glanced up and smiled at Beth from the outer circle as to be part of the team moment, but he became lost in her. She looked game day ready in a clingy black fast-skin racing suit. Her tinted goggles sat on her forehead, above her sun-tanned face and clear, pretty, brown eyes.

Beth stood facing Andrew and the team, her silhouette backlit by the banner-ridden scoreboard, in front of a school building with its locked closed doors. As if hypnotized by Beth's seashell earring spiraling in the sun, Andrew pictured himself walking into school in the morning, opening a locker near hers. He pictured himself sitting with her in the hallway, sharing one ear of a pair of headphones, singing Maroon Five.... And she will be loved.... And she will be loved.... He saw himself holding her hand walking her to class; and then, right there at the end of the day, he was sitting with her on the steps underneath the library window facing the stadium, right there ... sitting close to her, near her, breathing in the Vanilla perfume of her fragrant hair. He wondered what it would be like to lean in and have her eyes turn to meet his. He wondered what it would feel like to pull her close to him; and what it would feel like as her lips meet his.

Suddenly, Andrew's chest felt as if it was about to explode.

Beth's deep brown eyes met him in a surprising moment of contact, as if she had felt his daydream, and had pulled away from Andrew's stolen kiss.

Andrew managed an awkward smile before darting his eyes downward to the safety of the pool deck. Lost in his embarrassment, as if caught guilty in the act, he dropped his hands to his knees.

'130,' he thought feeling his heart rate surge in embarrassment. Andrew relied on his arms to keep his knees from buckling as Pat went on.

"Caz, you are in next." Andrew listened to Pat going on.

"OK, Pat man ... but are you sure you wouldn't rather stay with our normal order?" Caz replied.

Andrew caught Caz's dagger glance, and the poison tipped weapon struck its mark.

"You swim after Beth today Caz; Best effort from you today, too. Can you find a personal best today Caz?"

"You know I'm gonna try Captain."

Andrew, already in overdrive, choked back his breakfast, as Caz shifted his glance away from him in disgust.

"PB's all the way around we might have a have a chance," Pat went on.

"Pat, man that still leaves us like three seconds behind, and with Levine anchor for the Mustangs ..." Caz added.

"I know, I know, it's going to take a miracle," Pat said, "but today we have Andrew."

'Oh, no really?' Andrew thought to himself, as he stood rubbery legged in embarrassment by a failed stolen kiss, and a mind full of doubt and unchecked fear let loose by the dagger of emotional poison.

Pat looked into the pack.

"Andrew ... Andrew Galloway. Come up here."

"OK guys, make some room ... Andrew is new to the area, and will be with us in those hallways come September," Pat pointed to the school beyond the Sports Complex.

"And he's fast!" Pat called out. "Andrew is going to anchor," Pat announced formally.

'Great,' Andrew thought; 'just great.'

Andrew felt all eyes turn to him as he left the security of the outer circle and walked forward on cue. Andrew moved through the crowd in a full sweat, with legs like jelly.

"Excuse me," he said as he dipped his shoulder and held his head low as he brushed past the sophomore and junior swimmers on the outside of the pack, sensitive to, if not a bit embarrassed by the fact that he had just got ushered to the front without earning his spot.

Andrew approached Pat and Beth as he waded through Caz's glare. Caz's stance, look, posture, and facial expression all said 'Go Away.'

'I wish I could!' Andrew thought, chest exploding in embarrassment and humiliation, as he made his way to the front.

"Hey y'all," Andrew offered in his best Texas drawl.

Andrew stood in the huddle with a feint smile on his lips, shoulders slumped, and a look of worry on his face. 'I knew what I was feeling, but what was I thinking?' Agreeing to this … what a mistake. I am not sure I can make it down and back without getting DQ'd, let alone swim all out; what if I begin to cramp up. I am not even in form to go a personal best. What am I even doing here … competing again. After all I did to walk away. Mr. Mendonhall was right … I am in no shape to win a summer club meet, and that is exactly where I am. And what's worse, I am swimming for a team that doesn't really want me. And, I am replacing the captain of the team at anchor no less … not first, not second, but anchor! All because of a girl I just met!'

"OK guys, bring it in," Pat stretched his arm out in the center of the circle at the block. "Let's do this!"

Caz's left hand quickly topped Pat's hand. Beth's hand followed over Caz's hand and when Beth's hand touched Caz's hand their eyes met. Caz held the eye contact with Beth briefly without the response Caz was hoping for. Before Andrew could join the solidarity of hands, Caz quickly guarded Beth's hand by placing his right hand over the top of hers. Andrew placed his hand on top, over Caz's hand, and their eyes met briefly.

"Don't screw this up yo" … Caz jabbed shoulder to shoulder with Andrew, clustered in the tight huddle.

'Don't screw up,' Andrew mused to himself … like don't false start and don't miss the turn … like I just did in warm-ups. Andrew bounced up and down on his left leg hoping the twinge was gone, knowing he would have to flip at the wall for the second fifty. Andrew fought back the nausea of the moment triggered by the memory of whipping his legs over his head only to push out against an absent wall followed by a feeling of mortification. He could still hear Mr. Sebastian, "it's OK son, every racer has known that at least once in their career."

'Please not today,' he thought as he stood there, heart beat accelerating a bit faster now as he circled the blocks with the wave of weakness still coursing through his veins as nervous energy sapped his power.

———

Meza Sports Complex

12 Noon

"Swimmers to the blocks please; swimmers to the blocks," Andrew heard the muffled echo of the PA system. Andrew saw Beth scamper up to the block, making a last minute adjustment to her dark blue tinted goggles. She looked back from up on the block, but Andrew could not see her eyes.

"Here," she unclasped the sea shell spiral pinned to her ear, "hold this till I get out please," and she placed the spinning circle of silver into Andrew's hand. Before Andrew could protest, Beth was in the water.

Andrew stood poolside, squeezing Beth's earring, staring into the silver seashell that formed a concentric circle of smaller and smaller rings winding to a focused center. His pulse was racing now; his body was in a full sweat like he had just gotten off the track.

'What if I do false start' … he imagined, remembering how he felt when he saw the red 'DQ' flag flying over his lane the last time he false started and had been disqualified.

"Way to go Beth!" Andrew heard Pat shout.

'What if I get off the block and get to the wall and miss the flip; and what's worse, what if I get past the wall and I and don't have enough kick left,' he thought remembering the feeling a burning chest from air starved lungs and muscles locking up with lactic acid seeping into his arms and legs.

"She's keeping it close Caz," Pat said to Caz, as he waited poised up on the block.

'I can't swim like this,' Andrew muttered to himself fighting back the urge to vomit. 'My head's not right,' he knew, thoughts spinning, heart racing, guts churning; weak arms and legs sapped of nearly all energy with less than a minute to go before he was to be in the water. 'I am right back where I left off.' Meza, California, the city or state didn't seem to matter. What appeared to be safe clearly wasn't. Andrew met himself in the moment, and was disgusted. He saw himself stooped, hands on knees tasting the sourness of his gut in his mouth. With perspiring hands, he dropped the spiral earring, which bounced once before landing upside down. Down on one knee, Andrew picked up the earring reading the inscription on the back. 'Face Your Fears.'

Andrew looked up immediately into the stands. 'Mr. Sebastian,' he thought. That is what Mr. Sebastian used to say. 'No-mind is no doubt. No-mind is calm confidence. Face your fears, and see them as False Evidence Appearing Real, and you come to discover they exist only in your mind. See them for the illusions they are and release them.'

'Face my Fears Mr. S. Do I even have enough time? Face my fears,' Andrew thought. 'Look at me, I am even afraid to face my fears,' he thought.

Andrew went deeper into the glistening spiral as if in a meditative contemplation. The noise around him became blocked out as his focus intensified.

'My fears ... my fears,' he thought. Knowing it was the easy part, he realized. Saying it out loud was the tough part.

'OK, here they are ...' he said to himself. 'I am afraid to dive in that water and put myself out there again. I'm afraid I will choke ... false start, miss a turn, slow down, and cramp up, give out. I'm afraid we are going to lose and it will be because of me. And what I am afraid of even more than losing is that I don't have what it takes.

Maybe I am just a coward. There it is, the plain and simple truth. I am just a coward. And after this swim, everyone in this town will know it. Beth will know it; Pat will know it, every coach in the stands will know it. Even my mom will see me fail. And I'll be exposed ... exposed for the coward that I truly am.'

Andrew gasped, choking back the acid coming up from his gut, and stared deeply into the glistening spiral.

'There they are,' he thought, surrendering to the deepest feelings erupting from his gut. 'OK, you win,' he said as if talking to a foe with no name, no identity, but real enough to own his strength, and energy. 'So be it,' he said, looking deeply into his mind's eye, confronting the demon of doubt.

'If I crash and burn, so be it,' he thought with an honest acceptance of his fears in such a vulnerable moment of truthfulness.

'If I crash and burn, I'll deal with that,' he thought to himself, a psyche beginning a transformation.

'But no way am I not going to compete today' ... 'I may not win ... but I am going to fly ... ' he said committing to a certain resolve.

'Best I can is all I can do,' he said feeling as if the negative repressed energy dissipate out of his system like compressed air escaping from a release valve.

'I'm going to leave it all out there,' he told himself,

moving up subconsciously tapping into the power that existed in his personal code of honor.

'If Thorpe found it within himself to go 1:44:06 over two hundred meters, I know I can do a hundred under 55, even if I am not peaked. After all the time I have spent training, I should be able to do at least that.'

"Sometimes the best way out is through," he said out loud, into the spiral of light in his open hand. "Heart then head, and 'no-mind'."

Andrew gathered his energy, emerging from within the contemplative state induced by the spiraling earring.

'I had to come back, didn't I, Mr. S? I had to come back to take on the demons. I can fold up and go away or find the courage to take them on headfirst. Either way, I can't run from them any longer. I guess Mr. Mendonhall was right about that; winning does take courage. It's today's glitch in the Matrix, Mr. Sebastian,' Andrew said silently looking into the stands. 'It's time to take on the Matrix.'

'Heart then head, and 'no-mind',' Andrew said to himself. "OK, I'm all in," Andrew said out loud.

Andrew closed his eyes and went over his swim in his head. He saw himself leap off the blocks, far and high leaving sound behind as he entered the water. He saw himself streamline in a powerful kick-out. In his mind's eye he began to swim, powering through the water. He saw himself, staying within himself, pacing as to not burn out too quickly on the first lap. He saw himself hitting the black "T" before the wall, and then taking those last two strokes before the flip. He visualized a flip turn on the wall, a lunge followed by a pull out. He saw himself staying with pace for the first two strokes off the wall before unwinding all out for the last lap. He visualized a strong finish and a final lunge to the wall stopping the clock. "Heart, then head, and no mind," he thought.

All in, with a plan in place, Andrew focused on his breathing, preparing for the effort to come. With doubt removed, with his fears faced, it would come down to effort.

As Pat had predicted, Beth touched at 59, and gave Caz the pool in third place. Andrew saw Caz lose ground in third falling further behind. Andrew tucked the silver seashell into the nylon of his waistband and he broke the seal of his goggles that had formed a cloudy film in response to the humidity bubbling up from the frothy, blue, chlorinated, water. He sifted the fog away from his goggles in a quick rinse in the water before quickly securing the eyepiece creating a secure suction. He stepped up on the block feeling the gritty sandpaper-like texture of the two-foot by two-foot starting block. Andrew reached forward leaning in, hands gripping the platform that tilted slightly at a downward angle. His body tensed gathering combustible energy as he prepared to explode off the pedestal, a good 3-seconds behind the leader in the final one hundred meters.

In the blink of an eye, waves of white foamy water lapped into the wall of the pool in eddy currents, and Levine was gone: off the block, out in to the air and in to the water in lane three.

"Close this out, Levine," he heard in the background.

"Fifty meters there, fifty meters back, Levine, flat out … PB baby, meet record!"

'Perfect there, perfect wall, and then perfect back,' Andrew thought locking the program into his mind's eye, gripping the starting block platform at a downward tilt like a crouched sprinter in the blocks ready to explode as soon as Pat touched the wall.

"Come on Pattie-boy; get in there and touch!" Caz shouted emphatically on the pool deck hanging on to the chrome legs anchoring the starting block to the floor, embarrassed by giving up ground during his leg of the relay.

"Come on P, pull, pull, pull!" Beth exhorted leaning in over the water, off to the side of the starting block.

"Way to close Pat! Way to close!"

"Look at that," said Caz with Beth on the other side

of the starting block, "we are going to put the rook right there ... any one of us would be able to close that gap."

Beth roll her eyes at Caz, disgusted, before she said, "Even if Pat closes that gap, who do you know that can catch Levine, Caz?"

"Come on Pat, pull, close – last twenty five!!"

In a staccato of shouts into the water, encouraging lane three, Andrew sensed the crowd's excitement as the staccato of shouts over the water crescendoed as the swimmer in lane three hit the water. Andrew knew the crowd anticipated the victory to go to their favorite.

"You got this Levine!!"

"Bring it home, this is ours ... go, go, go!"

Andrew watched time tick away in increments of one one-hundredths of a second as the golden bulbs on the scoreboard clock marked time as Pat pulled closer to the wall. Andrew waited for Pat to touch and he felt as if time was slowing down while his awareness was speeding up. The last two seconds of Pat's approach seemed like two hundred.

Andrew felt as if everything around him was moving in slow motion. Quiet seemed to replace the cheers and exhorts of the pool deck. His senses were alive and he could feel the sandpaper like texture of the starting block under his feet, the tension of the goggles on his face and the flex of his legs and fingers as he loaded on the block ready to explode into the water.

At the moment of release, Andrew exploded off the blocks. He leapt high into the air, driving his tucked head up and flinging his flexed arms into extension, first up to his chest then exploding up over his head, the fibers of his muscular arms and shoulders fit and trained from mornings in the water and on the track, and afternoons wrestling the handlebars of a flying dirt bike. He arched his spine extending forward in midair and then kicked back with his legs like a spaceship powered by a booster rocket.

The sun highlighted his short sandy brown hair with radiant streaks down the parted center. In midflight high above the whitewater lapping into the wall of the pool behind him, Andrew felt calm, confident and relaxed. In the slow motion quiet of deafening silence he felt as if he was riding a ray of light. Gliding high in mid air, in the state of no mind, body poised with potential energy, he waited for his task to begin. At the apex of his leap, the laws of physics caught back up to him, and he felt gravity pulling him down. With his hands clasped overhead, arms straight and strong he pierced the skin of the water like an arrowhead, streamlined and fast as time began again.

"Go, Go, Go!"

"Come on Four!"

"Kick it up Four!"

"Go Andrew! Go, Go Go!"

After a long submerged glide, Andrew gave a powerful undulating thrust of his torso, hips and legs. He pulled down to rocket out of the water like a submerged dolphin gracefully negotiating the resistance of the ocean currents leaping up to the ocean surface, as he emerged from the kick-out 75 meters left to go. He was now only two body-lengths behind.

"Lane 4 made up half a body length just on the dive!!

"Hey who's that in lane 4?"

"Did you see that start?"

"No one is going to catch Levine – the kid's too good!"

"Not gonna do it!"

"The kid can't catch their ace – gap's too big."

"Might be close though!"

"A come-from-behind victory for the Championship?"

"Would be a great story if happens!"

After touching the wall Pat raised his chest and torso up to the pool edge, and quickly swung his leg over the deck top, raising himself completely out of the water.

"Good job Pat!"

"Thanks sis – how far?"

Pat flipped off his goggles and did a 180 looking back at the size of the deficit.

"He went in about 2 and half body lengths behind, but made up half a body length on the dive alone," Beth reported back.

Andrew did not hear the madness in the stands; he did not see the spectators gathering closer to the pool's edge to see what was to come in the water battlefield. The buzz of shouts, whistles and the din of excitement were lost in the churning water, flutter kicking legs and hands that tossed fistfuls of water aside with each clutch.

"The rook will never be able to catch Levine," Caz chided Pat.

"I don't know," Pat said smiling, "let's see what kind of heart this kid has ..."

Andrew looked up through black rimmed goggles with a rubber white headband and saw bubbles fluttering ahead, like the propeller of an outboard. The flickering bubbles of Levine were ten meters ahead of him. With a few powerful strokes after his pull out Andrew made up more distance. He headed to the wall in rhythm, breathing every eighth stroke efficiently pulling towards the wall.

On the pool deck, Amanda Galloway pulled her Polaroid into ready position. In front of her wearing a press badge, that said 'Stenger' stood a pear-shaped man of 40 with stubble for hair.

"Nicky, come over here," she heard Stenger say. "We got ourselves a race here!"

"I see it Sten, let's get a closer look" – said his mirror image in the crowd.

"This kid is fast! Who is he? I never saw him before have you?"

"You know, he reminds me of this kid I saw a few years ago in New Jersey swimming 15's; he won the free and fly at the East Coast Conference indoors. I think he went to California to train, but I had heard he was a burn out ... pot head I think ... left swimming ... Callahan or something like that."

"No Callahan in the program. Why didn't we see him swim any individual events?"

"He's fast, but Levine in lane 3 is no slouch – he is the Texas State Champ; won the fifty and the hundred here last two years running: And that's who they came to see," he pointed over to college row.

"Oh, is that the kid who made Junior Olympics last year?"

Pat watched Andrew's wake trail behind him in the

water like he had watched Andrew in the Mesa on his dirt bike when a wake of dust and sand trailed the rear wheel of his motorcycle. Pat was struck by the scene … Andrew was like an extension of the bike that day, standing tall over the handle bars, pulling the nose of the two wheeler up onto its rear, touching down only to fly up the broken ravine ramp, motoring and flying around the wild landscape. In the water, Andrew had that same style. He seemed to meld into the water rather than attack it going as fast as the water would let him go.

"Why'd you let him swim last Pattie; You can take him in a hundred straight up; you coulda put him first, or after Beth – then it would have been me and you like always with a chance for the title!"

"Sorry Caz, but this was our best chance for the team to come home with the title. I put Andrew at anchor because it was our best shot at winning," he said admiringly, watching Andrew approach the turn on the far side of the pool.

"Today its Beth, then you, then me, then Andrew," Pat said, and he turned his attention back to the water. Andrew was about to flip for the last 50 home.

Beth watched shoulder to shoulder with Caz and Pat, with Andrew still 1/1/2 body lengths behind Levine twenty meters from the turn.

"He's too far behind," She worried out loud to the two of them.

"See Pat, I knew the kid would screw it up," Caz leaned in.

'Lane three is too fast,' Andrew's awareness reported, after his body swam the first 30 meters. 'He is too fast for me to catch him at my pace,' Andrew knew. 'Sprint it' ... his awareness brought forth the solution.

'If I sprint all out this early I will give myself enough pool to catch up. But ... I'm going to risk burning out too early.'

Andrew easily recalled the feeling of arms too heavy to lift out of the water, and the cramps underneath the pit of his arms that accompany swollen legs, aching for oxygen, that eventually lock up. If he sprinted too early he risked losing: losing time, losing speed, losing ground, and being passed up.

'I know that if I get there, I can hold on,' he thought as his turnover increased. 'It's only a hundred.'

In the space of eight strokes, Andrew pressed for more speed. He kept his head down, chin tucked, fingers cupped and fanning the water only to enter again in a ballet of speed, precision, motion as his turnover increased and his legs kicked it up to a higher gear.

With his chin on a swivel in the pit of his right arm he maintained his rhythm.

"Go Andrew go!! Pull! Pull!"

"Come on Andrew, you can catch him!"

"Go Andy, Go-oo Andrew!!"

Andrew's feet produced propeller-like bubbles and the distance closed as he headed to the turn. Across the lane dividers he was a body length behind the swimmer in lane three when Levine hit the turn for home.

"Fast Wall Andrew!"

"Blow it out!"

"Kick it!"

"Move it!!"

"You think he can catch him?" remarked Beth.

"I doubt he can hold this pace … He's going to burn himself out Pattie!" said Caz.

"You might be right Caz," Pat said, "let's see how much heart he has."

Submerged in effort, Andrew clicked along in his programmed pattern gliding through the water. Pull, lift, paddle, paddle, paddle, breathe; pull, lift, paddle, paddle, paddle, breathe, blowing out a stream of expired breath through his nose; a trail of bubbles expanding away like the wake left from an outboard motor. In the fixity of effort, Andrew only heard the sound of his own breathing. He marked the wall and prepared for the turn.

"Who is this guy?" asked Cal's coach.

"Not in the program." Responded the coach from U.T. "But this first fifty is going to be better than good."

Andrew ducked his head, tucked his chin, threw his legs powerfully over his head then gathered in a tuck and then exploded off the wall as if he was trying to break the plaster. After an undulating glide his feet whipped up white water as Andrew passed by the swimmer in lane five. Completing his kick out Andrew began to turn his arms over, faster and faster just as his mind had programmed him to do.

"I got lane three at 26."

"Lane four is in around 24."

"Either of those fifties makes my team...."

Midway in the last lap, Andrew felt the burning in his chest, as if there was smoke deep down inside his lungs. His ribs expanded further desperate to take in more air, but he maintained the discipline of his swim ... a single breath on only every eighth stroke.

"He's locking up Pat, I told you he would burn out," Caz stated midway in the final lap.

"He's holding up just fine ..." Pat replied.

"Can't do it ..." Caz hoped.

Twenty meters from the finish, Andrew had pulled to within a head of the leader. He was peripherally aware of the stream of water trailing the nose from the red-capped opponent when he pulled in his last breath. He kept his head down, and pulled, no breath, no extra movement that could slow him down. Streamlined, body centered, Andrew pulled with his arms and pounded water with his legs, all out. In his effort to increase speed he was starving his body of oxygen. Kick, kick, stroke, stroke; kick, kick, stroke, stroke, his lungs collapsing down as he expelled his remaining breath in a continuous pattern of exhalation. His thighs burned from the lactic acid that had accumulated in his muscles over the last 80 meters and he fought against them locking up. Five meters to the wall, less than two seconds left to touch a pad that would stop time, stop a clock and take a breath!

"He's going to run out of pool – he can't make it!"

"He's locking up!"

"I don't know, he's closing. Can you believe it?"

"Come on Kid!!"

"He's going to come in Second!"

"Last twenty meters and still behind!"

"They're going to touch together!" As they stared at the wall in a flurry of white chlorinated white water.

Below the surface of the water, Andrew reached out in a final lunge at the black electronic circular sensor attached to the wall, stopping his lane clock. He glanced to his left, and saw Levine touch at the same moment he had.

Amanda Galloway, Nicky, Stenger, Beth, Caz and Pat all acted in unison with the eyes of the fans in the stadium. All eyes darted up and away from the water to the scoreboard hanging high above the pool. To the naked eye, it was a dead heat. The touch appeared simultaneous.

Above the water, there was an explosion of applause and hollers as the times were posted. Lane four's time read 3:42:22 and was flashing a one after the posted score. Lane three's time read 3:42:23, in second place.

After touching the pad and stopping the clock, Andrew exploded up into the air, like a dolphin surfacing from a dive. "Great swim man," Andrew heard as Levine who was leaning over the ropes thumb up, palm open, looking back at the clock congratulating Andrew. The two shook hands as if they were arm wrestling over the lane ropes.

"Thanks, you too," said Andrew from lane four.

Andrew stared up at the clock, wondering how time could possibly be divided in that small of a measure.

"Ahhhh," exclaimed Andrew, almost falling back into the water, exhausted as he pulled himself out of the water, some how managing to stand up back to the edge of the pool, somewhere just beyond the limits of his own physical power and endurance.

"Way to go Andy!" rushed Pat, smiling; palm open, grabbing Andrew's right hand in recognition of the triumph. Pat's embrace spun Andrew and he could see Caz turning, walking away, almost disappointed they had won.

Off balance, spinning to his right by Pat's acknowledgement of the amazing, in a brothers-in-arms moment, Andrew felt two hands on his shoulders tilting him back to his left.

"Oh my God, you did it!" Beth said as she rushed to him.

Reflexively, Andrew welcomed her approach with his free left arm; the fragrance of her hair, already etched unmistakably in his mind, once again in range. Quickly, he felt her inside the space of his body, her hands on his shoulders, tipping him to her. He felt her face press to his cheek. Aware of her, with the feel of her body pressing into him, he felt a soft kiss delivered to his cheek.

Andrew's awareness hung suspended, as though the simultaneous events were singled out. He was aware of the sweet fragrance of her hair announcing her arrival. He was also aware of how he held her, left arm wrapped around her waist; aware of the thin film of water skidding off her nylon racing suit separating her skin from his: aware of her lips on his cheek, soft, the contact so unexpected, yet so welcomed.

Andrew was not aware of a flash of light behind him, subtle, lost in the bright daylight sun, and Andrew did not hear the winding drone from yesterday's technology.

Andrew was not aware of the crowd, or the coaches or Stenger or the Polaroid, as he remained lost in an embrace and a kiss as sweet as a dream.

Held upright by the power of Pat's grip, hand-to-hand with his own, pulling him back on balance, a flurry of lights began. The pool deck was soon overrun by the influx of friends, family and coaches freed from the stands.

In that moment, Andrew felt more than pleased. It was as if he had conquered a demon that guarded a great treasure. Somehow the challenge had left him a bit more courageous. It was as if he had gained a new level of prowess by speeding through time and water, pushing past exhaustion, posting a good time and winning a race; a win that even Mr. Mendonhall might approve of: a win, in the heat of battle, in the matrix when it counted most.

The swim was thrilling no doubt. However, there was a moment following the swim that was as powerful even if unexplained, unsuspected, unprovoked: the rush of her wafting Vanilla hair; that magnetic attraction that pulled her into his arms, the essence of her form merging with his followed by an unsuspected kiss: a kiss as sweet as a candy. Who would believe that he did all that for a kiss? But that kiss was worth it … and he'd do it all over again in a heartbeat. Although it was over quickly in time, Andrew felt like it was somehow forever … the kiss and the feeling of her, and that moment now permanently etched into Andrew's awareness was deeper than a memory. Andrew knew he walked away changed. He walked away as if knowing he had met his destiny.

Tomorrow's *Meza City Journal* would run an article on the meet, entitled,

"A Hero in Time!"

The cover photo would be an electronic version of Stenger's photo. The photo caught Caz full on, walking right toward the camera arms up in celebration. Pat and Beth were lost behind Caz, and barely visible in the photo. And Andrew; Andrew was nowhere to be seen. But the article did mention that a stand-in swimmer came off the bench to anchor the relay with a fifty-two second final one-hundred-meter swim, in a come from behind victory bringing home the 2004 Championship for Meza Valley swim club.

"Caz," Andrew said smiling as he read the article and looked at the picture ... "Figures."

Andrew could not help but replay the day's events one more time. He knew the real story would never be told. The story about the inner demons he met earlier that day; and that surreal moment in time high over the water where he felt like he was breathing in the energy of life. No, nobody would ever know about that. And that ending; that was really something! And as if thinking about it again made it real, Andrew touched his face trying to feel her lips touching his cheek again.

Andrew's mother flapped the wet film and watched it materialize with a sigh. Amanda Galloway caught the back of her son, gripping a high five with his teammate while receiving a kiss on the cheek from the pretty teammate she saw Andrew fixated on.

"How could I get the back of my son in such a moment of triumph?" She sighed, feeling as if she missed the shot.

"It would have been a nice post to the refrigerator door," she said. "Oh well, at least I was there to see it," she told herself, looking at the Polaroid.

"She *is* pretty," Amanda said holding the Polaroid, admiring what she knew her son had been admiring.

Amanda Galloway placed the Polaroid in her bag, and the photo eventually found its way on top of Andrew's laundry the next day along with a note. Andrew smiled when he saw it. He pulled the picture close to his nose, and breathed in the wafts of vanilla that he could almost sense. He opened the note, and smiled.

"I have a party to go to tonight," he said with the hope and promise of what was yet to come.

CHAPTER 14

———

Monday Night July 2, 2012

Steward Township Hospital ICU

17:00 pm

Ginny, in navy blue scrubs with a crew-neck collar and cargo pant style bottoms walked around the small space of ICU bed-1.

"Well ... you've put in quite a long day today Sister," she said as she flipped her long, dark red ponytail around her neck as she ducked under the silent TV bolted to the wall facing the foot of the bed. She unwrapped the facial dressings, took down the 2x2 gauze dressings covering her patient's swollen eyelids and was met with a pair of emerald green eyes.

"You!" TV 14406 said into the ET tube, looking up into the eyes belonging to the nurse with a shock of red hair, tied loosely together.

Ginny saw his eyes dilate, as if he was processing visual information, and then constrict again. "You!" Ginny said, stepping back on guard, as if she saw a ghost.

"Oh my ...!" Ginny said spine tingling. "Can it really be?"

"What's wrong my dear?" asked Sister Mary Grace still seated in the chair facing the patient in the bed.

"I've seen those eyes before Sister! I mean I've seen him before; but ... can it really be?"

Ginny paused frozen still, placed her hand up to her scalp and felt the deep scar well hidden under hair. She looked down at his eyes which seemed to look up at her, staring at the memory of her past as if it was right in front of her again today; the memory of a pair of deep green eyes staring at her through blood, cracked glass and rain.

"Do you know him my dear?" Sister Mary Grace asked.

"Yes, I think so Sister, but no ... not like that. I don't know who he is exactly," Ginny said, stooping over her patient to get a closer look at the unexpected arrival with no name, no identity. Ginny stepped back around to the tray table. She held the Polaroid up and looked past it, then back to it, as if comparing the likeness of the face in the photo with the shape of the head in the bed.

"I know you," said the eyes of TV 14406 to the girl at the window studying the Polaroid. "The ravine; Thunderbird."

"No help," Ginny concluded as she studied the two male figures in the Polaroid.

"That night in the rain!" TV 14406 said while craning his neck like a horse trying to break its tether, pulling at the ET as it attached to the ventilator.

As she held the picture in front of her, Ginny saw her patient turn his head quickly and forcefully, as if trying to find her in the room. The sudden movement dislodged the tube from the ventilator.

"Code Blue, ICU-1, Code Blue ICU!" the overhead paging system rang out as the Ventilator alarm sounded immediately.

Ginny quickly reconnected the tube as Dr. Williams arrived on a jog responding to the rapid response in ICU- bed 1.

"What's going on Gin?" Dr. Williams asked surveying the room.

"He tugged on his tube. I think he woke up for a moment and got agitated."

Williams quickly assessed the patient. "Looks pretty sedated to me; ET looks good, he said; getting O's ... Dr. Williams said referring to Oxygen. Cancel Code Blue," Dr. Williams said into the intercom.

"Code Blue, all clear. Code Blue, all clear," the overhead rang out.

"Oh Gin are you crying? Gin what's the matter?" asked Dr. Williams pulling a tissue from the nearby dispenser. "It's all right it's not your fault or anything."

"I think I might have spooked him."

"Spooked him? What are you talking about?"

"I don't know, its just that well he opened his eyes you see when I changed the dressings over his eyes … he was staring straight up at me, into my eyes and, well I'm not sure, but I think maybe I know, I think maybe he knows…. Oh I don't know, I thought for a moment that when he opened his eyes, he recognized things, you know and maybe even people."

"I doubt it Gin. He is out. He's not processing anything, Gin."

"It's just I thought for a moment that when he opened his eyes, he recognized things," Ginny said.

"Like me …" she whispered to herself.

"Listen, I'm going to finish rounds and then I'll be back to check on you, OK?" Dr. Williams said winding his stethoscope up into a coil and placing it in the back pocket of his scrubs. "Oh, and Gin," he said looking backwards at her as he paused in the doorway. "Good save today."

"Thanks," she said, not fully engaged in her smile. "But that's just it," she said after he had already left the room. "I think it is the other way around. I think he saved my life," Ginny said to Sister Mary Grace who had observed the event from her bedside chair.

———

August 27, 2004

Meza Texas

2100

The ranch was across the railroad tracks west of Thunderbird Mountain, where the land began to flatten out into the mesa. The sandy ravines and desert landscape had been in Caz's family for years, and the single road that led to the ranch, was not paved. Caz's family had started and stopped converting the ranch into a resort, with the early plans for a golf course laid out in the valley beyond. A narrow river formed the property's southern border as it flowed southwest down the valley guarding the last property in the county. The barn and stables had been gutted, but construction had stopped at the framing. For the soon-to-be seniors at Meza High, the barn was a perfect place to throw a party.

Saw horses with plywood tables were set up in front, at the center and out by the back entrance. Two big fans were set up on the far tables and a beer keg on ice in the middle table sat guarded by red solo cups. A long orange extension cord hung over the rafters and supplied power to the fans and a spot light over the keg, all powered by a portable generator in Caz's truck out back. Caz's truck was joined by a row of tailgates of the many truck beds that lined the back lot. Each tailgate was down, some were lined with blankets and cushions to sit on, some pumped music, all tuned to the same station. Music found its way into the building, which was nothing more than leaning posts created by the studs, and a wide open dance floor.

From just inside the back entrance of the framed barn, Andrew spotted Beth walk in the front door. He made a move to make his way over from his spot at the back door to the entrance across the room, but he was trapped by the crowd that was growing around the keg in the center of the room. He merged into the outer edge of the party that flowed around the keg like a traffic circle, and began the trek around the outer edge all the while spotting her as she walked as if away from him.

From within the center of the circle, Caz saw Andrew spot Beth, and plotted a course to intercept him. Caz made his way from the center of the room and cut a path like a spoke from a wheel center, walking to the outer edge where he made his way to Andrew, who still had better than half the room to cover before Andrew could reach Beth.

"Glad you could make it rook!" Caz said meeting Andrew's eyes, while he spot-checked Beth's location across the room.

"Thanks for the invite," Andrew replied.

"Now you've only been in town a short time right?" Caz asked Andrew.

"Yes, about two weeks." Came the reply.

"Well great. Let's introduce you to some people then!"

Caz threw an arm over Andrew's shoulder and began moving him back to where he came from, around the circle away from Beth.

"Let's hang here for a moment," Caz said, and he pushed Andrew back into an open door frame that must have been meant to be a closet or a bathroom, plywood surrounding him on all sides. "I see part of the welcoming committee."

Caz reached into the crowd and pulled out two pretty girls with brown hair, red lips and short skirts with boots and each wearing a halter-top. Except for the color of the tops, Andrew could not tell them apart.

"Lizzy, Lucy, come here," Caz called over and put his arm around the neck of one of the twins pulling her in. Andrew saw Caz spill some beer down the halter-top of the girl in blue, pretending as if it was an accident. Wet, the halter clung to her breasts leaving little to the imagination.

"Caz ..." Lizzie pulled back the blue strap a bit to mop up the spilled beer, watching Andrew's response.

Caz watched Andrew's eyes as well to see if he took the bait.

"Lizzie, you and Lucy have got to welcome our new classmate. This is Andy, I think you saw him today at the swim meet, didn't you?"

"We sure did, right Luz?"

"Uh hum, you looked marvelous," said a nearly identical Lucy in her yellow halter-top.

"Why, girls, your beer cup is empty" … and with a quick hand gesture from Caz, two full cups of beer were passed forward.

"Two beautiful girls like you should not want for anything here tonight… Mi casa es su casa," Caz handed them the full cups. "Isn't that right Andy?"

"Yes, sir," he said, nodding politely at the girls, eyes up as to not demean the introduction.

Lizzy and Lucy guzzled the beer in tandem, then laughed as if on cue.

"So we can have anything we want tonight Caz?" Lizzy asked holding out her empty cup.

"Does that include any*one* we want?" asked Lucy with a giggle, raising an empty cup up, shoulder leaning in batting her eyes at Andrew.

"Maybe, maybe … let's see," said Caz.

"But first, how about more beer?" Caz had two more cups in their hands immediately.

"And you …" Caz checked Andrew's half-full cup, "you are like the guest of honor tonight, Andy. Drink up! You are sipping at a snail's pace. The girls here are putting you to shame!"

Caz got three new refills this time, and watched the

girls guzzle their beer, while Andrew barely sipped either of his two cups.

"Oh, Caz," Lizzie kidded, "we can out drink and out dance any of you macho types!"

"You're right, Liz," he said. "We need some music to really get this party started!"

"Dee" … Caz called out to the black haired boy guarding the speakers, "load it; you know, the song …" Caz watched as the DeeJay, the master of tunes for the evening, loaded in Caz's request.

"Ozz, Birdman!! Here!! Bring it in!!" Caz shouted calling the group to a huddle.

"DeeJay … Spin it!" Caz orchestrated the scene. Ozzie, Caz and Byrd broke out in song … singing, arms interlocked shoulder to shoulder….

"We are the Champions,"

"We are the Champions,"

"No time for losers 'cause we are the champions…. of the World…!!"

As the song finished, Caz yelled out, "Shots!!" and he pulled Andrew in by a hoarse collar hug … Caz filled a beer cup full with whiskey.

Ozzie and Byrd each took a shot, and then passed the half full cup to Andrew.

"Down it rook!" Caz laughed.

Andrew took a sip, and passed it along–

"No way ... this is your shot, rook; You gotta shoot it; after all you are one of us now."

Reluctantly, Andrew downed the cupful of whiskey, and was immediately sandwiched between the twins as a dance song spun out next from the large speakers.

"Come on dance with us," pushed Lizzie.

"Oh don't be shy. It'll be fun," pushed Lucy.

"Not really much of a dancer," Andrew said as he sidestepped hoping to get out from between the two girls, while trying to survey the far side of the room.

"Don't worry we'll show you," Lucy pushed into him, until he was stopped by Lizzie behind him.

Before Andrew could squeeze his way past the guarded doorway, Lizzy was bumping and Lucy was grinding, each singing the 70's classic,

'I ... Love to love you baby ... I Love to Love you baby....'

"Oh, hey Lucy, you and Lizzie, are both really nice and all, but ..." Andrew did his best to wiggle free, but with no luck.

"Oh silly, I'm Lizzie – can't you see I'm wearing blue!" And with that she pulled the front of her top forward, like showing off suspenders, sure that Andrew would see all she had to offer.

"And I'm wearing yellow!" Lucy quickly snapped

yellow straps forward showing off more than just the tan lines below her triangular yellow top.

Andrew quickly looked up taking his eyes off what the girls were happy to show off. The girls laughed catching Andrew's blush and reddened face. Andrew felt penned in. Caz laughed at the scene, well pleased with his handiwork, as he caught Beth locked on Andrew and the twins from across the room.

From across the room Andrew felt the weight of disappointment. He could feel Beth's eyes on him as she stood with her friends taking in the twins burlesque-like routine. Penned in to the closet like framing, with the girls chest bumping and hip checking him in the tight space, he felt their hands on him.

Suddenly, a flash of lightening turned the room momentarily dark, and the crowd moaned in unison. Andrew pushed past the form of the two girls breaking out of the framed pen like he was bursting through saloon doors in an old western.

When the lights came back on, the spot at which Andrew had last seen Beth was empty, and she was nowhere to be seen.

"Hey rook, come back here!" Caz said, stepping in front of him with Ozzie, all six foot six of him. The two stepped blocked Andrew from going any further.

"Hold on rook … don't think you should be driving, given the beer and the shots and all."

"Oh Caz, let me …" said Lizzy, and before he knew it Andrew was being groped from behind by one of the sisters who proudly pulled a set of keys from Andrew's front pocket.

"Better take this too," said Lucy, hands emerging from Andrew's back pocket. Lucy handed Andrew's wallet and phone over to Caz.

"Mighty nice of you to contribute some funds to the party!" Caz pulled the cash out of Andrew's wallet and tossed the rest back to Byrd.

"After all … no drinking and driving! Dee-Jay! Got some more keys for you," and Caz tossed Andrew's keys and phone over to Jay across the room on top of the large speakers. Andrew saw Caz laugh as Jay caught the keys but dropped the phone.

"Oops…" said DJ, as he dropped kicked the phone back toward Andrew through a puddle of beer and melted ice.

"Hey Byrd, better go load Andy's bike in the truck … he won't be driving home tonight."

No phone, no keys, no money, Andrew stood sandwiched between the two sisters behind him and Ozzie and Caz in front of him. A moment later, the barn lit up bright again, and then the room went dark and the music stopped. This flash of lightening was followed by the deafening crack of thunder and the barn began to reverberate with the sound of falling rain. In the blackness Andrew broke free of the girls and slipped past Caz and Ozzie. He swam through the throng, taking the long way around the circular crowd, but could not find her. He searched the back entrance, toward the golf course, scanning the line of trucks, but did not come across the orange jeep. Out toward the line of taillights and closing tailgates, Andrew heard line of truck engines fired up. Headlights blazed across a future golf course, and one by one the in crowd peeled out in single file toward the only road out.

Before he knew it, Andrew heard the unmistakable sound of his dirt bike turn over, and saw the single light of his dirt bike guided up the ramp of the Ford Super Duty by Ozzie and Byrd, as DJ rode shot gun and Caz revved the engine.

"And there it goes," he said, watching the Ford Super Duty with his bike in the back, turning off the road, in the front of the pack of exiting cars and trucks turning into the valley of the would be golf course.

Andrew knew he had to go after his bike. He locked on to the taillights of the big Ford and he began to trot behind the truck, quickening his pace moving deeper into the night as the truck struggled in the uneven and unstable, wet terrain.

Rain quickly followed the crack of thunder and large drops pelted his face as the Texas weather unleashed high winds that managed to grab the heavy drops and move them sideways. The downhill pitch of the valley carried water through the mesa turning the ravines into quicksand. Running now, Andrew was gaining on the truck. The fog lights attached to the roof of the cabin gave his target a distinctive silhouette and Andrew kept moving in the direction of the lights. He heard the wheels of the 4 by 4 spinning out and he saw the forward progress of the truck stop.

As he approached the truck, Andrew saw Byrd and Ozzie standing in the payload.

"Cut that bike loose," Andrew heard as the engine of the dirt bike came to life inside the truck bed of the Super Duty Ford. Andrew began to run faster as he watched Byrd let the tailgate down, while Ozzie rode the bike into the wheelwell, cracking the headlight of Andrews' bike trying to turn the bike from within the truck bed. With the bike facing out towards the tailgate, Andrew saw the big Ford accelerate; when the nose of the truck caught some traction, the idling dirt bike began to move forward.

When Andrew saw his bike being launched from the bed of the truck he began racing in a full sprint. With a running start, he bounded up onto the back wheel well, and leaped up in the air. He caught the handlebars of his bike in midair, his momentum righting the sloping bike. He deftly threw his right leg over the seat and hit the footplate gaining control of the machine in midair. He pulled up hard on the handlebars, depressed the clutch and waited for the bounce to come as he and the bike approached the terrain below.

"Oh snap ... did you see that!"

"That was like spiderman dude!"

Ozzie and Byrd watched in amazement. They saw this shadow appear from the blackness deep within the night leap into the air, and grab a moving machine, land, pop the clutch and wheel off into the night.

Relieved to be on his bike, Andrew searched for a way back to the barn. If Beth was still there, he wanted a chance to to explain. Andrew's instinct took him off head first into the wind. There was no road and it was very dark. With a broken headlight, in a rain that seemed to come from all directions, Andrew was not sure if he was going to the barn or away from it. He moved slowly in the darkness, maneuvering though the dunes, fighting the rain and quicksand-like ravines like an expert skier through moguls on a mountain, until finally finding a single lane road. Unsure if he was travelling to the barn or away from it, Andrew looked up for help from any recognizable landmark when he saw a pair of headlights approaching. He recognized the dim headlights as a small pick-up truck, and saw the truck being blown around in the wind. The truck was all over both sides of the narrow lane and Andrew realized that the driver would not be able to see him as he had no headlights. With the small truck only twenty yards in front of him, Andrew pulled up on the handles of the lightless dirt bike lifting himself off the road into the gully as the small truck passed him. With a sigh of relief, Andrew watched the truck travel forward, away from him. He must be traveling the wrong way, he thought, and he pulling a one eighty, spinning around. He began to follow the small truck that had almost taken him out.

Out of the gully, back on the road Andrew opened up the throttle trying to get close to the truck, hoping to share it's headlights. Andrew trailed the small truck by a thousand meters when he saw the big Ford bear down the center of the one-lane road.

As if in a game of chicken, the big Super Duty came bearing down on the little truck closing the gap between the two quickly.

A horn blasted and the bright headlights blazed over the cabin and began flashing right before the blinding flood lights came on. Andrew watched the small pick-up pull hard to the right to let the Super Duty truck pass. Andrew watched the pickup catch the edge of the gully and career off the embankment where it flipped over on its side. Just as the pick-up went into the gulley and flipped, Andrew pulled off the road, catching air landing in the gulley. He travelled in the gully along the side of the road racing toward the flipped pick-up. Concealed in the gulley, Andrew saw the Ford Super duty pass on by. Andrew rode in the ditch beside the road until he came across the small pick-up truck and it's sole occupant in the cab of the truck. The young, pretty red-haired driver was covered in blood that streamed down her forehead from a shard of glass in her scalp. Andrew caught her pretty face full on, locking eyes for what seemed like an hour, before the blood forced her eyes closed in less than a minute.

"Help me, please," he heard, "I can't get out. I'm stuck! I'm stuck!"

Andrew stepped back, surveying the scene. The truck had turned sideways. The driver was the sole occupant, and she was semiconscious, but in a panic, as her arm was pinned and she hung suspended by the seat belt.

"OK," he said, "you are good where you are! I am going to get you out." Andrew ran around the truck and started rocking the pick-up: pushing it then pulling it trying to get his body underneath it. From the passenger's side, Andrew began pushing and pulling and rocking the cabin until he had lifted it high enough to squat underneath it. Flushed with adrenaline, with a guttural grunt, Andrew used all the strength he had to push the truck over.

Andrew jumped in next to the pinned victim, and he moved her to the passenger seat. He seat-belted her in; then he took off his shirt, and used it to pull out the shard that had pierced her forehead. He used his blood soaked shirt as a headband-like wrap to suppress the bleeding.

"I got you, you're OK," he said. Andrew searched for a cell phone in the cabin, but there was none to be found. He tried the ignition on the pick-up, which turned over after three cranks. "Look ... we've got to get you to the hospital quickly. Which way? Which way do I go to get back to town?" he asked, realizing that he was not going to get back to the unfinished business at hand in the barn. But his passenger sat there quiet and still, incapable of answering, eyes mostly closed now beneath the head dressing, concussed, bleeding, and exhausted from the panic of the ordeal.

"What's your name, he asked her," as he pulled the small truck out of the ditch on to the single lane road. Andrew's companion mumbled something inaudible as she quivered in tears.

"I bet they were heading to town," he said and he directed the truck in the same direction of the Ford.

"Hang on, I got you," he said checking his semi-lucid passenger in the front seat as lights came into view from the valley below. "There's a hospital down the valley. I had to drive by it every morning on my way to the stadium. Hang on; see those lights, there? That's it! Hey, wake up; try not to sleep. Hey tell me your name!"

Andrew sped away to the lights of town and found the highway. Fifteen minutes later he pulled up to the ambulance bay of Steward Township Hospital and lifted his passenger out, running her into the ER.

"I need help, please," he said to the nurse manning the triage post. "I think her name is Virginia…. She was flipped over in her truck," he explained as a gurney found its way to him.

"We'll take it from here," said a nurse. Andrew watched the scene from the bright lights of the double doors to the ER. Within minutes, he saw oxygen placed by prongs in her nose, and an IV was in. Before he could move, she was off down the hallway with three attendants on either side of her.

Shirtless, with rain and blood-soaked blue-jeans Andrew breathed a sigh of relief. He turned facing the closed double doors of the ER and began to walk out. The doors would not open, and he flashed his hand across the sensor, and said, "Open Sesame." But the doors stayed closed. "Young man," he heard a moment later, "Please come with us, we have some questions for you," said a man in a uniform with a badge that said 'Sheriff.'

The triage nurse handed Andrew a towel and he was quickly escorted in the opposite direction, behind the glass doors of the ER.

"Have you had any alcohol tonight, son? We got a report of an incident son, involving a drunk driver and a stolen vehicle."

"Great," Andrew said to himself. "Just great!"

CHAPTER 15

July 2, 2012

Steward Township Hospital

1900

Simi walked with his head down toward Williams filing through papers before stopping at bed-1.

"Figures," he said.

"What's up Simi?" Williams responded, checking monitors and lab results.

"We might have a positive ID on TV 14406 in bed-1 there; seems he has a record; arrested in 2004, DUI and attempted auto theft."

"Oh, yeah?"

"Apparently the charges were dropped ... seems like he agreed to join some military program ... probably to avoid doing jail time would be my guess...."

"Explains the paratroopers," Williams responded.

"Great, let Jill know as soon as you can confirm the details. She might be able to track down some family."

"Will do. In the meantime, I told Losha to keep him breathing and feeding … brain might be bad, but organs are good … just in case. Does Dr. Mac let the second years scrub in on organ harvesting?" Simi asked Williams.

"No organ donation going to happen here, Simi. He looks too good. Just write for the titration please, and let's see how he looks on rounds tomorrow. We might be able to extubate him tomorrow."

'Note to self,' Simi thought, 'write orders to titrate paralytics and sedatives before I sign out tonight. Don't want to screw this one up,' he thought as he walked out of the ICU.

———

July 3, 2012
Steward Township Hospital
ICU
0600

With long auburn hair wearing dark blue scrubs Nurse Elizabeth Mackenzie paused in front of the magnetic doors to the ICU. She swiped the screen of her mobile phone and pressed the quick dial and waited.

"Hey, it's me," she said after the beep. "Call me as soon as you get this." The nurse depressed the red button and swiped the screen closed. 'Still going directly to voice mail,' she reflected with a sigh, placing the phone in her cargo pocket. Elizabeth released the magnetic door to the ICU with her photo ID badge and walked toward the main desk.

"Well, well, well! Miss Elizabeth!" Miss Marge said to the auburn-haired nurse from behind the desk at the nurse's station. "Mission accomplished so soon? I had you out all week Elizabeth."

"Hi, Miss Marge," Elizabeth said to the charge nurse. "Yeah, I guess I am back a bit earlier than I planned. Hey, I am Cindy today, do you mind writing me in?"

Miss Marge sponged the dry erase board wiping out the name 'Cindy', and posted 'Beth' with a blue dry-erase marker.

"There … now you are officially here!"

"Thanks Miss Marge," Beth said checking the board. "Oh, I'm right across from Ginny," she said. "Better stop in tell her I'm back."

"Ah, yes, you better. And by the way, will one of you please walk Sister Mary Grace in at seven? She's probably already in the family room down the hall from the unit waiting to begin God's work."

"Will do," replied Beth.

Beth walked down the corridor of rooms in the ICU stopping at bed 12. The collapsible chart station of bed 12 was down, but no Ginny.

―――――

0615

Ginny stepped back into ICU-1 again and warmed her bare-skinned arms that were raised in goose bumps as her intuition tingled with excitement and concern. She couldn't be sure … but something inside was telling her it was him; even though her memory of that night in the rain was cloudy, the picture of the emerald green eyes of her rescuer had been imprinted in her mind like a branding iron into flesh. Something inside told her that the green eyes in bed 1, opening from time to time, were the same green eyes of her rescuer from that night in the rain.

Ginny rifled through the cargo pants on the tray table by the window and pulled out the Photo and began studying the Polaroid for any additional clues as to the identity of TV 14406 with the familiar emerald green eyes. Ginny took a moment to study the details of the Polaroid. There were three people visible in the action photo. Two of the three figures were male, one with his back to the camera and one caught on profile. It was hard to get a good look at the faces of either of the men. Of the three figures in the photo, the most striking subject was the female. Her profile was clear and focused. Ginny's spine began to tingle again.

"Oh my God!!" Ginny said, standing bolt upright,

putting her hand over her mouth. Ginny stuffed the parachute under the cargo pants, and placed the photo face down on top of the tray table. With beads of sweat on her face, she turned and walked out of the room.

————

0620

"Ginny must still be in report," Beth thought, checking her watch in front of the empty nurses station. She poked her head in ICU bed 12. The room which was occupied by a fortyish male with an arm in a long cast and a long rod securing the bones in his leg from moving. The nurse recognized the external fixator, but did not see any signs of Ginny.

"Hi," she said. "Just looking for your nurse."

"She went across the hall; I think Bed-1," came the reply.

And with that, Beth turned, went back out, and walked directly across the hallway into ICU bed-One.

"Oh, hey Gin!" Beth said in surprise, as Ginny appeared to be fussing with a dressing that encircled her patient's head like a mummy. "Do you have Bed-One? I must have misread the board. I thought Miss Marge assigned bed -1 to me?"

"Beth!" Ginny turned immediately pulling away from the patient, "what a surprise," Ginny said as if seeing a ghost for a second time in two days. "What are you doing here? I thought you were off all week ... well this week ... and you are not supposed to be and here you are and I was ... I was just ... no but...."

"Good to see you too, Gin!"

"No ... it's just I didn't expect it to be you.... I mean I didn't expect you ... and here you are! Well then! Did you have a good time off?"

"Well, it was definitely an adventure; I'm not sure how good it was. I'll have to tell you about it over drinks some time!"

"I thought Miss Marge put you in Bed-Twelve?"

"Yes, and no, no, he's not, I mean I don't have this one ... I mean Cindy has him."

"Cindy called in, holiday and all ... and Alice caught me on my cell. Since my plans blew up, I thought I would work today, take my mind off things a bit."

"Oh, OK, then ... well here you are, here, I mean dressing needed adjusting, so I, that was all I was I ... so ... so he is all yours," Ginny stumbled on.

"Gin its no big deal, if you have already assessed him we can switch assignments. I'm sure Miss Marge has more green dry erase markers at her desk."

"Oh, no, yes, I mean yes, you take bed 1 he is yours. I'd better get back to my guy in Twelve."

'Strange,' Beth thought to herself, as she watched

Ginny scurry off to bed 12, 'it's as if I caught her with her hand in the cookie jar.'

Beth surveyed the screen, monitors and tubing. Everything looked secure. Her patient had facial dressings wrapped in an abundance of kerlex, but he looked stable, covered under a freshly pulled clean white sheet. Standing by the empty bedside chair immediately adjacent to the door, Beth scanned the room, which otherwise looked in order.

"What in the world is that doing here?" Beth said walking to the tray table next to the bed. Beth picked up a packed parachute that sat neatly folded, along with a pair of cargo pants and a tattered tee shirt on the tray table by the window.

Beth stepped outside, grabbed the clipboard, and walked back into the room, taking a moment to read over the hand-off report from the night shift.

TV 14406, a no information patient injured in a motorcycle accident: sedated, satting 95%, heart rate and blood pressure stable through the early morning. Split facial skin, protected by moist dressings and two by two's over closed eyelids had just been changed.

"Think they used enough Kerlex?" Beth said to her mummy, staring at her patient's head that was nearly completely covered by white Kerlex wrap.

Beth looked out into the hallway, across the corridor and made eye contact with Ginny, in ICU Bed Twelve. Ginny looked over at her, tilted her head and made a facial contortion as if to say, 'So what do you think?'

"Too much," Beth mouthed, picking up the half used roll of white Kerlex wrap. Ginny had been one of her externs, and Beth was glad that she had chosen ICU nursing after the time spent together on her rotation. Beth stood smiling, and Ginny motioned back cryptically, as if Ginny was waiting for something more from her. Beth shook her head, from outside the window of ICU-1.

"Not sure what you mean," Beth mimed.

Beth moved quickly about the room and intermittently glanced across the big window separating her from Ginny. Every time Beth looked up, she was met with Ginny's quizzical expression and cryptic hand motions.

"Boy, Ginny's sure acting strangely today," Beth thought.

Before leaving the room, Beth folded the parachute, along with the cargo pants and singed tee shirt, gave one last look at the monitors, and fluffed the bedside chair, primping it a bit.

"Hey, Gin; Miss Marge asked one of us to walk Sister Mary Grace in. I'm heading over there now, OK? I will be back in a minute. Will you listen in for me?"

"Sure thing," Ginny said.

———

0645

"Did an alarm go off Gin?" Beth asked surprised to see Ginny back in ICU bed-1.

"Oh Beth!" she said, eyes wide-open, pupils dilated, as if she had seen another ghost.

"Everything all right, Gin?" Beth asked as she walked arm in arm with the nun making their way to the bedside chair.

"Uh, no, yes, I was checking … checking to make sure all was quiet, you know…. Good morning Sister," Ginny said in a loud voice.

"Good Morning my dear," Sister Mary Grace said bowing; her robes billowing out as the pleats expanded, the white inner band of her black head wrap worn like a headband. Sister Mary Grace sat in the bedside chair, fumbling with her rosary beads out, listening to the two nurses banter.

"You walked over to see if all was quiet, Gin? But that doesn't make any sense?"

"Was Dr. Williams here, Gin?" Beth asked, her face lighting up a bit.

Sister Mary Grace looked up and gave Beth a wink and a smile, slowly pulling each bead from her waistcoat pocket, enjoying the soap opera above her.

Ginny looked down at Sister Mary Grace, but her face wore concern rather than embarrassment. She looked down at the Sister, and shook her head, "No, Dr. Williams hasn't been here yet today."

The nurses paused their exchange and looked down at the Sister.

"Now don't you two worry or fuss over me. I will sit and pray ... use my connections," she said with a smile and pointed up to heaven.

"OK, Sister, you go get'em," Beth said.

"He's all yours Bethie," Ginny said. "I better get back to my guy in Twelve." Ginny walked out of the room, and rubbed the skin trying to calm down the goose flesh still raised on her arms.

———

08:00 AM

After the medical team rounded, Sister Mary Grace settled in to a deep contemplative State. Deep within prayer, in a profound state of joy, Sister Mary Grace of Souls felt it happen again, even though she did not know what 'it' was. She felt her spine tingle and she felt a wave of energy climb up her spine to her chest where it centered. She felt the energy collect in her chest, and then flow out of into the world.

The feeling was brief, but the profound joy was lasting. In tears, Sister Mary Grace wept a prayer of thanks, before dropping her head in sleep.

————

10:00 AM

From outside the hallway, Beth was drawn back into the doorway of bed-1 by the beautiful hypnotic melody being sung in perfect pitch and timing.

Make me a channel of your peace.

Where there is hatred let me bring your love.

Where there is injury, your pardon,

And where there is doubt true faith.

O master grant that I may never seek

So much to be consoled as to console

To be understood, as to understand,

To be loved as to love with all my soul.

For it is in giving that we receive,

In pardoning that we are pardoned

And in dying that we are born to eternal life.

"That was beautiful Sister. We are lucky to have you."

"And you are an angel my dear" she said. No wonder he can't keep his eyes off you."

Beth's smile faded as soon as the alarm sounded.

"Code Blue, ICU; Code Blue ICU," the speakers blared.

Beth looked down at her patient who had managed to rotate his covered eyes and wrapped head all the way around as if looking at the Sister in the bedside chair, listening to the song of St. Francis. In so doing, he managed to disconnect the tube from the ventilator.

"Not on my watch," Beth said, quickly reconnecting the tube and called off the code, just as Ginny jumped into the room to investigate.

"It's OK Gin. I don't think he likes that tube. He keeps turning his head to look over this way; looks like that connection is not the greatest."

"Yeah, he did that with me yesterday when I had him."

"His eyes must really be burning Gin," Beth said noticing drops of fluid falling off his face like tears, soaking the protective dressings covering his face. "Time to unwrap that face and change those bandages."

"Beth, before you take down those dressings, I've got to talk to you. Beth ... It's important," Ginny began again.

"What's going on Gin? You have been acting strangely all day!"

"Well your patient Beth, ICU-1 ... I might have seen him before."

"TV 14406? The No Information Patient – you had him yesterday didn't you?"

"Yes, I had him yesterday, and there is something strange, Beth."

"Strange? Strange how Gin?"

"I think I might know him!"

"What? You know him?"

"Well yes, but no…."

"What do you mean, 'Yes but no'?"

"Well I think I have seen him before, but even though I've seen him before, I don't actually know him … I mean I don't know his name. But I think that you might."

"What? What on earth makes you think that I would know his name?"

Ginny was almost in tears as she stood face to face with Beth, while Sister Mary Grace stood across the room.

"What? Jeez, Gin, what's going on with you today … tell me what's going on?"

Ginny grabbed Beth, and walked her back to the unit clerk stationed directly across from the patient rooms.

"It was a long time ago at the end of summer. I had just turned sixteen. My brother let me take his pick-up out that night to celebrate with my friends, and I was going to pick him up at a big party out by San Jacinto, where they had started building the golf course. The one lane road was dark, no lights and the weather had turned terrible. I could barely see, and I was frightened, I felt like the wind was going to blow me off the road.

I was almost there, when I saw a big truck coming at me. I thought it was coming straight for me hogging the middle of the road. I remember the sound of the blasting horn and the bright headlights and cabin lights flashing me. I pulled over hard to the right to let it pass, but I caught the edge of the bank. Before I knew it I was in a ditch beside the road. The truck had turned sideways and I was suspended, bleeding badly from a deep scalp laceration pouring blood over my eyes. My arm was pinned and I could not release the seat belt and I thought I was going to die.... When all of a sudden, out of nowhere, this motorcycle jumps over the truck and lands in the ditch. I see this guy – with emerald green eyes peering in at me. Things are a bit fuzzy, but I remember his eyes; he started rocking the pick-up: pushing it then pulling it trying to get his body underneath it. He kept coming around to check on me, and I remember the feeling as I looked into his emerald green eyes. From the passenger's side, he pushed and pulled; I saw him move it high enough to squat underneath it. He must have pushed it over but I don't remember much after that. I remember waking up in the hospital. A few days later I went back out towards San Jacinto, his bike was still there. The front rim was bent. It was covered in mud. It looked liked it was abandoned. Then the other night, this guy comes in, and ... I swear I am looking at those same emerald green eyes that I had seen before."

"What? You think this patient is the guy from that night? The guy that saved you in a ditch? What would be the odds of that?"

"I know Beth, but I think it is him."

"Did you ever find out who he was?"

"No, but Beth … you should sit down for a minute…."

"Gosh Gin, really? What is up with you today?"

"Beth, there's more…."

With her back to the outside window, at the tray table across the bed facing the two nurses, Sister Mary Grace smiled while studying a Polaroid photo wrapped in a protective coat of scotch tape. Sister Mary Grace looked down at the photo as she held it in her rosary bead wrapped hands, and then she looked up, smiling at Beth. The Sister looked at Beth, looked down at the picture, looked up again, and then looked over to the masked patient face up in the bed. Sister Mary Grace looked up at Beth one more time and said,

"Ahh, he loved you from the moment he saw you, my child!"

Beth, stood in the doorway between Ginny, smiling at Sister Mary Grace, unsure what was going on. She just laughed, playing along. Sometimes the Sister was eccentric, she understood, and Beth did not always know what she was referring to.

"Yes, Sister," she smiled, not wanting to embarrass Sister Mary Grace.

"Pretty as a picture," Sister Mary Grace said as she turned the photo around.

Beth reached over her patient in the bed, and took the picture from the nun. Her finger caught the pin of a heart shaped earring, securing a note behind the Polaroid.

"Beth, That's you isn't it? There. That's you in the photo right!!" Ginny ran over and stared over Beth's shoulder as Beth studied an old Polaroid photo.

Beth saw herself caught in an embrace with a young man whose back was to the camera. She recognized her brother in the photo as he was caught mid-swipe in a 'high-five' with the young man. Beth saw her younger self, caught flush on recoiling, but still held within the stranger's arms. Beth recalled the moment exactly.

"Yes, that's me … very funny Gin. And, I can't believe you got Sister Mary Grace in on the act!"

"This is from the summer before my senior year, at Championships. That's me, and Pat … and you are not going to believe who that is right there," she pointed to the figure with his back toward the camera. "That is Andrew!"

"My goodness, I've never even seen this photo before. Gin, where did you get it?"

Beth studied the photo, when realization lit across

her face like a detective studying the forensic evidence at a crime scene.

"Wait, this is a polaroid Gin! It's an original. Someone had to be there to take this."

"Where did you get this Sister," Beth asked again, "Is this a joke Gin? Are you two playing a welcome back joke on me?"

"Beth, that's the other thing I wanted to talk to you about. This picture ... it's his ... I found it in his pocket. This guy with the familiar green eyes was air vac'd in with this Polaroid picture in his pocket ... a Polaroid of you."

"Him! With this ... and a picture of me?" Beth's smile faded, and her stare deepened as realization took the place of amusement.

"Bethie," Ginny paused tensely, "We also found a note; it was zipped up in his pocket along with the picture and the earring."

"What?"

Ginny handed her the note, and Beth saw her own handwriting. 'Dive Shop, July 4th ... Be There!'

Beth studied the details.

"No, that can't be. No, it can't...."

Beth reeled, taking a step back. She looked down at TV 14406, face wrapped beyond recognition ... body covered in compressible air pumps, draped toes to neck, floating on a big blue air mattress.

Beth flipped the wristband of her patient … no name, only a number to identify the patient in the bed.

"It can't be," she said, still confused. "He is at The Dive Shop. I spoke to him on the phone, two days ago."

"Beth, have you spoken to him since you got back?"

"What? Well no, I've been calling him over and over since I got back but he's not picking up – but you know how the cell service can be. I keep calling but … I bet he is waiting for me…. We had a date – July 4th, The Dive Shop.

Beth peeked under the Kerlex wrap trying to discern his features. She lifted the moist gauze from his closed swollen eyelids and her face lit up like a Christmas tree.

Below the moistened gauze, a pair of emerald green eyes peeked through burnt, blistering skin that had already started to peel.

"Andrew!"

CHAPTER 16

July 3, 2012
Steward Township Hospital ICU
1900

The energy output of worry weighed heavily on Beth as she replayed the whirlwind that was the last 13 hours. Beth arranged for another nurse to cover her shift, and Ginny spared Beth the pain of handing off her patient to the resource nurse who assumed care of Andrew. Beth met with Jill in Social Services and together they had contacted Andrew's mother who was on her way to the hospital. Andrew's father was still in flight completing his assignment. He would be there tomorrow.

Before going back to the ICU to sit with Andrew, Beth stepped into the nurse's locker room to change and freshen up – at least put on some clean scrubs before meeting Andrew's mother. Tears flowed again as Beth anticipated the conversation that needed to follow; a conversation that Mrs. Galloway deserved, and a conversation in which Beth planned to explain her role in her son's calamity.

Hoping Andrew's condition had improved since she was last in Andrew's room, Beth walked down the hall of the ICU, eyes fixed on the door of bed-1. Before entering, she folded down the collapsible chart rack and accidently knocked the chart to the ground. The clasps of the three-ring binder broke open as the chart contused the floor with a bang. Beth looked around, embarrassed, and said "Sorry," and began collecting the sections that had scattered trying to reorder the disheveled mess. Ginny immediately emerged from bed 12 at the sound of activity.

"It's just me," Beth said fighting back tears working fastidiously on the floor.

The clack of the falling chart broke through the quiet, and Sister Mary Grace returned to consciousness. She looked around, but there was no one in the room with her other than the patient. The metronomic beep sounded a predictable pattern and the corresponding bleep marched across the monitor above signaling ongoing life as she sat vigil at the bedside of Andrew Galloway. Sister Mary Grace smiled at the life beside her; she saw him open his eyes and turn his head toward the sound of noise and light. "It's almost time," she said.

After reassembling the chart and collecting herself, Beth entered the room, surprised at the sight of Sister Mary Grace.

"Sister Mary Grace, what are you still doing here?" said Beth checking her watch.

Sister Mary Grace smiled and said, "I am just sharing a moment with this young soul. Sometimes Presence is the best gift we can give."

Beth looked at the nun who appeared much different than the vibrant Sister she picked up this morning. Her face was gaunt, and she looked pale. Dehydrated Beth thought.

"You look exhausted Sister! Have you eaten? You have probably already missed dinner at the residence. Come on, Let's go over to the cafeteria and get you some food," Beth said hooking the nun's arm and walking toward the door. But before they could make it to the cafeteria the lead changed and Sister Mary Grace pulled Beth into the family room and had her sit next to her.

"Come sit with me, my child," and she reached up to dry the still moist tears from Beth's face.

"Have you been crying all day my dear?" Sister Mary Grace held Beth's hand as tears streamed down her face and her mascara began to run.

"On and off ... all day Sister," Beth managed a tear mixed laugh and unfolded her Kleenex tissue.

Ginny entering the room marking the end of her shift, quickly sitting on the other side of Beth on the three-person sofa seat in the family room. Sister Mary Grace looked deeply into Beth's brown eyes, holding her gently, supporting her with a warm smile of deep concern. Sister Mary Grace picked up the Polaroid examining it in her hand, glancing up to Beth.

"The memory must be an emotion deeply cherished, for him to hold it so dearly."

"Oh sister … I don't know how could that be, really. I mean our beginning was really bizarre. I knew him briefly, like for two days at first, but then…."

"Ahh, you loved him from the moment you saw him, didn't you my child?"

"Well, I guess, at first, I thought he was cute. We didn't really talk at all when we first met. You should have seen him, really, he was kinda tongue-tied … but still cute. But I guess I knew even back then, by the way he looked at me, Sister … that he liked me. And I used that against him sister," Beth told with a smile. "When he stood in front of me, at Championships, the day of that Polaroid, with those big green eyes … he didn't hear a word I said. It was like he was lost, this big puppy dog. And I used that against him. I asked him to swim for us, and I knew he would do it for me: I know he did do it for me. I was the reason he was there. And that is where the

Polaroid was taken. After he won the race. My hero....
Afterwards I guess I felt responsible ... so I invited him
to the party after the race that night. And I have to say;
I was surprised by how excited I had become knowing
that he would be there. I thought that we would really
get a chance to talk, and get to know each other. But that
never happened. When I arrived to the barn, there he
was – the big star – dancing with Miss fast and her twin
sister Miss loose. And even though I knew I shouldn't be
hurt, I was. I felt like he was my find ... you know, that he
should have been paying attention to me."

"And then," Beth went on, "just like that he was
gone.... Andrew Galloway was just gone. He just disappeared as fast as he came. Never came back to the pool
to train, I never saw him cruising around town, and he
never showed up for school ... just gone."

"I thought about him from time to time," Beth said,
"but when the weeks passed into months I got the feeling he was gone for good. Nursing school followed college for me. And I began working resource, and I really
enjoyed working as a preceptor for the younger nurses.
They had a mandatory girls night out at the end of every rotation, and just before Christmas, last year, when
I least expected it ... the past came back to say hello."

———

December 23, 2011
The Sand Bar, Meza Texas
21:00

"Oh my goodness ..." Beth said to herself, as she sat in the dimly lit bar with a group of nurses from work. Surprise unexplainably gave way to anger, before Beth became excitedly curious over the unimaginable appearance of a pair of broad shoulders attached to a muscular frame with emerald green eyes. "Andrew!"

Andrew Galloway entered the Sand Bar and took five steps forward before stopping to let his eyes adjust to the dimly lit surroundings. The wooden floor smelled of spilled beer, and he could see whole bottles formerly containing whiskey and tequila decorating the tables. The room was alive with music, and couples danced up front, while a throng of patrons gathered in the back of the room at the long bar buzzing with the exchange of money for bottles and tumblers that splashed over before finding their way across the maple hardwood top to their new owner.

"She's supposed to be here somewhere," Andrew thought as he scanned the scene.

"Why Andrew Galloway!" Beth said to herself. "As if back from the dead." Beth bobbed her head hiding, unseen under the cover of her group, and she feigned interest in her girlfriends' conversation.

'Good crowd for a Thursday night,' Andrew thought feeling momentarily uncomfortable as he surveyed the room with a field agent's eye, noticing the bling and sparkle of belt buckles, boots and jewelry. Andrew knew he couldn't risk going home to change, and he reassured himself. He didn't want to risk missing her … didn't want a repeat of the last time.

"Oh he's got his good gym clothes on tonight," Beth chuckled, watching Andrew walk past the front door, wearing a red fleece Under Armor sweatshirt with a zipper for an I-pod in the shoulder.

Andrew unconsciously looped his thumb under the chain around his neck, and swiveled the earring-turned-medallion across and then back again as he circled the room from the entrance. Andrew's stare pushed past the vibrating sound from the band in the front of the room to a swivel at the end of a long crowded bar. Andrew saw a stunning face peak out from behind a circled group of patrons sitting on a few bar stools while others stood around her leaning in to the bar.

Good intel, Andrew thought.

Andrew's target quickly tucked in, and he lost her

in the cover of the group of girls, hovering around two barstools.

Andrew watched her cautiously emerge from the blind, take a quick peak around the room and then quickly conceal her face again. Andrew saw her head bob and move in laughs as her friends provided cover, watching for a sign of recognition as a glance grazed his fleece sweatshirt.

From his position, he could see the back of her head, her long chestnut hair flowing in straight highlighted lines, and he noticed she was wearing a white tailored shirt with dark blue jeans and boots.

'I don't think she remembers me,' he thought, catching another glance full on.

Andrew walked slowly, as if on recon, taking the long way from the door to the front of the room. Keeping an eye on Beth he proceeded around the room trying to remain unnoticed. Andrew walked and watched Beth. Sweat beaded on his brow as he noticed Beth swivel on her bar stool, as if conducting her own recon.

Andrew turned back to face the bar as he walked near the dance floor in front of the room. He noticed that Beth had rotated to face the stage. As he continued to the far side of the bar, he noticed her position had changed again as she swiveled the stool to face the far wall. Andrew completed his circle around the outside of the room and landed at the opposite side of the long straight bar catching Beth's profile as she swiveled the stool looking straight ahead at the dance floor. Andrew felt the glancing spot checks and he felt sure he was in her peripheral vision.

'Well,' he thought. 'The hunter is being hunted;' not sure how to interpret the maneuvers.

'Are you here to meet someone?' Beth thought as she watched him at the far end of the bar opposite of her.

'She either doesn't recognize me or ...'

'You are not talking to anyone,' Beth observed, as she dropped her head back and peered down the bar.

'Or maybe she recognizes me but doesn't want to talk to me....'

'Why do I even care?' She asked herself, unable to suppress the twinge of excitement that she felt.

'She doesn't appear to be here with another guy ... maybe a girls night out?' Andrew thought keeping his distance.

'Because you liked him, she admitted to herself. And you know he liked you ... and you liked that he liked you,' Beth told herself.

'Maybe I should just pony up and walk over to her and say hello,' he thought as he looked down the bar while he twirled the silver seashell medallion on reflex.

'Can't say I didn't wonder about you,' Beth thought as she took in his muscular physique and green eyes. Beth deftly avoiding his glance by tucking away, back into the crowd when Andrew leaned forward trying to see past the bar line.

'Can't risk it,' he thought, staring straight ahead at the dance floor, with a bottle of beer in his hand.

'I wonder if he is supposed to meet someone,' Beth thought.

Andrew scanned down the bar but his eyes met the girl next to him. "Oh, hi. Sorry, do you want me to get the bartender for you?"

Beth watched Andrew politely lean in and smile, then pull back away as if looking for someone.

'He is definitely on the hunt. Hungry like the wolf, Andrew?'

"Oh, no, I'm not waiting for anyone, not really, just here, you know, unwinding," Andrew smiled a social smile to the girl in the seat next to him as she engaged him in bar conversation.

'Oh, she wants more than a drink, all right', Beth thought, as the girl next to him reached across and touched Andrew's arm.

"Nice to meet you two," Andrew said, offering his seat after shaking hands with a second girl who had arrived to join her friend at the bar.

'Two at a time; as I remember, that is more your style, isn't it?' Beth thought, feeling a twinge of anger return.

"Who are you stalking, Bethie?" Cindy asked.

"Yeah, are you actually interested in a guy?" Alice added.

"What do you mean?" Beth asked her friends in feigned surprise.

"Him ... that guy; you are so totally checking him out! Don't deny it!"

"And I see him looking back at you!"

"Do you know him?"

"Oh Bethie, he's dreamy," Karlie jumped in.

"Go talk to him, Beth. If you don't want him we'll take him. Just go talk to him and bring him over here, OK? We can handle it from there! Right Soph?"

"Oh, I think the two of you would be perfect for him," Beth said with a mischievous grin.

"Time to have a little fun, girls," she said pushing

away from the barstool with a smile. "I'll be right back," she said.

'Oh, no, she's not leaving is she?' Andrew thought as he caught Beth walking behind the bar out of sight. Andrew tried to lean forward and break free from his interested new friends.

'Surprise attack,' Beth thought as she saw Andrew pulled back into conversation by the two girls at the bar.

Beth walked out of sight to the front of the room while Andrew stared at the exit sign in the back of the club.

The two girls at the bar went silent when Beth brazenly pushed past their prey. Beth leaned on the bar, approaching from Andrew's rear, as he faced the exit sign and the back of the bar.

'If she didn't walk through the exit, where did she go?' he thought. Suddenly, Andrew heard his two friends stop talking. Andrew then caught wafts of Vanilla floating up from behind him.

"Hi Andrew, win any races lately?" Beth said from behind him.

"Why Hello, Bhair" Andrew responded, off guard, spinning.

"It's Beth," she said with a playful huff.

"Beth, I'm sorry, I meant to say Beth, but I might have been … your hair you see … I mean … it's been a few years…."

"My friends are gawking at you," she said pointing down to the other end of the bar. "They think you are dreamy. Come on let's dance so I can make them all jealous."

Beth took Andrew by the wrist without waiting for an answer. She led Andrew to the center of the dimly lit floor. Andrew followed silently heart rate accelerating with each step forward, and the familiar fragrance of Vanilla wafting past him in her wake.

"Your hair, Beth."

"What?"

"You smell the same," Andrew mumbled as she led him forward.

"What?" she said feigning insulted surprise, and she turned her head back, with playful eyes and a captivating smile.

'You did not just say that, did you? Geez!' Andrew thought admonishingly.

"Did you just say I smelled the same? What, like chlorine and sweat?" she said.

"No, no, it's not that … it's your hair," he said sheepishly, "Vanilla. It smells … I mean I remember that about you."

Beth turned completely around now, facing him, looking up into green eyes widened by the dim light and fear.

"You remember my hair conditioner, do you? Thanks a lot. I can't tell you how many times I was hoping that I would meet a cute guy at a bar and he would tell me that he liked the way my hair smelled," she played with him.

"With a line like that you better be a good dancer. Are you a good dancer?" She pushed back, looking into his deep green eyes, smiling.

"Dancing," he said, "well it's not really my strong suit … but if you want to, I mean … I've come too far to turn back now … I mean we are already here and all …" he fumbled turning to face her, mesmerized all over again.

"Well, as I recall, the last time I saw you, you had no problem with the bump and grind. But we are not in a dark secluded barn now, are we? So why don't we start out with something more traditional," she said, "maybe like this…."

Beth squared up standing face to face with Andrew as the drums paced a slow beat. And before he realized it, his hands were holding her. Andrew began to sway side-to-side barely moving forward with his right foot as she turned him slowly. A flute softened the mood, and his heart skipped a beat.

The rhythm of the song was soft, making movement slow, but holding her made his world speed up. With slow steps and a heart beating quickly, Andrew enjoyed both things together at the same time.

Andrew turned with Beth in his arms, Vanilla wafts of fragrance like perfume overpowering the floor covered in whisky, tequila and beer.

Andrew kept his hands respectfully on Beth's hips, her body close to his, but not in contact, wanting to talk, feeling like he should speak. His heart was racing now, just as it did seven years ago when that kiss, out of no where left an indelible mark on his soul.

'You are as beautiful as I remember ... no better not say that,' he let the air dissipate from his rising chest.

'Holding you in my arms is a dream come true,' he filled his lungs up again ready to tell her. 'Can't say that,' he thought.

'Just dance,' he thought. Just her hold her and dance, he breathed in and out.

"Are you all right?" Beth asked of her silent dance partner breathing in gasps with beads of perspiration forming on his brow. Beth could feel his pounding chest despite their separation.

'Beth, I have thought about you every day for seven years,' he fought back.

"All good here," he said instead.

"All good?" Beth pulled back slightly, "You are a charmer, aren't you!" Beth said. "Well that's good … keep breathing big boy, don't ditch me out here on the dance floor like you ditched me at the barn the last time I saw you…. It's Beth, by the way … just in case you forgot."

"Oh, Beth … I could never forget…. I have thought of you every day since we first met," he said to her unable to censor his heart any longer.

'Oh no, I didn't really just say that did I?' Andrew thought panicking.

"Is that right," she pushed back. "Every day? What's that, now, like seven years?"

"Yes, every day. And you are even more beautiful than I had remembered."

"Thanks," she said into his serious deep gaze.

'That was genuine,' she thought. 'Authentic. He really meant that.'

Beth decided to not pull away. She let herself fall in a bit closer, taking away the two inches that had initially separated them as they moved slowly around the floor together.

'It was refreshing to see, really,' she thought. 'Honesty; no come-ons, no pick up lines … in fact that had to be one of the worst lines ever. But … he had remembered me. Every day for seven years?'

'My hair,' she smiled as she tucked her head down into his fleece sweatshirt.

The two slowly turned another circle as the music flowed fully…. "Two by two their bodies became one …" Beth sang the Madonna lyrics softly as Andrew turned her.

'He's sweet,' she thought; 'was then, seems to be now.'

Beth pulled up to look at Andrew. The light from the stage caught the spiral on the chain around his neck, and Beth recognized the spiral seashell immediately.

"What's this?" she asked him.

"Oh Beth, I wanted to return it to you. I wanted to give it back, but…."

"You turned my earring into a necklace?"

"No, I mean yes, I did, and it's yours if you want it … but it's the only thing I had to really remember you by. That and … "

"You kept it … to remember me?" She asked.

'He kept it,' she thought. 'All this time, he had kept it, and wore it.'

"Beth I have thought about you every day since we last kissed."

"Kissed?" she laughed in a smile. "Did we kiss? I must have missed that!"

Beth moved her eyes from the spiral seashell up to his eyes, and smiled.

"Did we kiss, Andrew Galloway?"

Andrew stood frozen still, like a deer caught in the headlights of an oncoming car. Beth placed her head back down on his shoulder and danced in his arms enjoying being held with tenderness. She flipped her hair, picked her head up and unclasped a single earring from the third spot on left ear. She unzipped the small I-pod style side pocket on the sleeve of his sweatshirt and placed the heart shaped medallion into the pocket.

"Here," she said, "hold this for me; hold this heart for me," and she placed her head back down on his shoulder, and allowed herself to fall more deeply into his arms.

Swaying and moving closely with him, Beth felt her heart beating, racing. He felt her sway and move with him, in time with the music, in time, in step.

Andrew smiled at her, and said deeply, from his heart, "I have been holding you in my heart for seven years now Beth."

Beth hesitated for just a moment; just to be sure. She didn't want to give herself completely away yet. But she was sure. His showing up here, wearing her spiral earring, the way he held her, and more importantly the way he looked at her. Holding on to a long forgotten kiss, holding her in his heart ... Beth looked up into Andrew's green eyes and saw the truth of his very soul exposed for her to see.

"Oh my ..." she whispered.

Beth turned on the dance floor with Andrew, stepping slowly, closer and closer. And with every step, she fell deeper into the meaning of his embrace, and she knew it was right. This tall handsome man, soft green eyes, smitten, thinking of her all these years ... and she did know ... she let herself hear what her heart had known after he left ... what her heart had known from that day ... she liked him. She caressed his broad shoulders, and she wondered about how many times she had thought about him. Andrew had been with her for a fleeting moment in time, and then gone ... and she couldn't help wondering what he was like ... what it would have been like if he had stayed.

"What in the world are you doing here, Andrew Galloway?"

"I had to find you Beth ... that kiss you placed on my cheek found it's way to my heart, and my heart would not let me rest until I found you again."

Beth dropped her head, embarrassed that a tear began to fall from her cheek. In her entire lifetime, she could not imagine hearing anything more powerful. What girl wouldn't wait an entire lifetime to hear someone tell her, no not just say the words but really mean it, really be the truth of it ... that their kiss found its way to a boy's heart, and that he could not rest until he found her again. He means it, she knew. There was no hiding that truth. She could just feel it.

'What would she think if I' ... Andrew thought to himself resisting the urge to lean forward and find her lips. 'It would be too forward....'

But Andrew moved his lips closer to hers anyway, as if drawn forward by a power from outside himself.

As she stood silently in his arms, she could feel his every heart beat with each breathe, and she was surprised by her matched response. She did not need to hear the words that asked the question ... but she knew what her answer had to be when he asked her,

"May I kiss you?"

Beth answered the question without words. She lifted her mouth up towards his. She parted her lips and closed her eyes in reply meeting his lips full on.

When Andrew's lips met Beth's mouth, he stopped moving. Together they stood as one, in a timeless embrace that lasted as long as one slow dance in time, but alive forever imprinted in consciousness.

———

"Oh my God, that little slut!"

"She's like making out on the dance floor with our guy!"

"A total stranger? That's not our Bethie!"

"He's no total stranger ... did you see the way they

were looking at each other from across the room. I bet she knows him."

"Hey, she was supposed to bring him back here for me...."

Beth's friends watched their instructor and their friend, in amazement, lost with Andrew on the dance floor. When the dance was over, and the kiss completed, Beth walked back to them, holding his hand smiling as if bringing back a prize. Beth led Andrew by the wrist, from the dance floor to the edge of the bar.

"Hey ya'll, this is Andrew," Beth introduced.

"Hello," Andrew replied to the group somewhat sheepishly, five pair of eyes sizing him up.

"So, Andrew, how do you know our girl Bethie?"

Chapter 17

"We saw each other every day after that until he left on deployment," Beth said walking Sister Mary Grace into the cafeteria.

"We were writing back and forth, talking when we could, but the service out there was spotty. Here, why don't we sit and I'll fix you a plate. Would you like a salad with the pasta?"

"Yes, dear, thank you."

A minute later, Beth returned with the tray.

"So how did you end up in Central America?"

"When the Caring Hearts Program planned a mission trip nearby I jumped at the chance. I always wanted to do something exotic like that; you know combine my nursing skills with an experience like that; and since Andrew was close by, we made plans to meet."

"So you never saw him, did you?"

"No, I didn't. It got a bit crazy down there. I had been calling and calling, but his phone kept going to immediate voicemail. This has gone so wrong, Sister. So wrong!"

"Sometimes my child, when many, many things go wrong something very special and beautiful is unfolding. We simply do not have eyes to see it."

"Beth!" TV 14406 shouted silently from the bed recognizing her voice. "You made it! Finally!" Andrew said in silence trying to turn his head to the window to look out at the beautiful crystal clear water.

––––––

June 30th, 2012
Central America
10 AM

Sitting on the bed in the small room of The Dive Shop Bed and Breakfast, staring out at beautiful crystal-clear water, Andrew Galloway recognized her ring tone immediately.

"Finally," Andrew quipped as he answered. "I've been trying to get a hold of you for two days now."

"Sorry," said the female voice on the other end, "spotty service up here in the jungle."

"Tell me about it!" Andrew understood the frustration first hand. Fading cell service had been common over the last six months of training in the mountains nearby.

"What's going on?" she asked.

"Guess where I am," he replied, looking at the crystal clear ocean water.

"Lying on a cot with collapsible wooden legs, in a tarp tent, somewhere up in the mountains?" The nurse had seen enough electronic images over the last six months to know what STATESIDE camp looked liked in the hills, not far from the Caring Hearts medical relief team. The mobile camp was completely knocked-down and would be folded up and put away by the end of this month.

"How'd I do?" she asked with a giggle, pulling her long brown hair into a ponytail and reapplying the scrunchy while holding the mobile phone under her chin.

"That would be about right if I was still up at camp. But, I got away early. I am staring at sand white like sugar that runs into crystal clear blue water that runs into the horizon of clouds."

"Andrew, where are you?"

"I am here; at the spot; at our rendezvous spot."

"You're at The Dive Shop?"

"I am indeed," Andrew said smiling into the phone.

"Well, as far as I know it's not July 4th now is it? I believe we were supposed to meet on July 4th, at The Dive Shop."

"I got away early; and I got us a room – ocean view."

"You got *us* a room? A *room*; as in one room – singular? Why Andrew Galloway, whatever in the world do you have planned for us I wonder," said the nurse in a faux southern accent.

"Oh, no well, I mean I just ..." he stammered, and she could feel his heart drop on the other end of the phone. Smiling, she let him simmer, wondering if his green eyes turned hollow like they did the first time she caught him in a flustered trap. After a silent pause, her brown eyes lightened and her lips turned into a smile. She cradled the phone and leaned in responding.

"Andrew Galloway, was 'a room' part of the plan?" she asked.

"Well ... I just thought that ..." Andrew stumbled, thinking about her, wanting to be close to her.

"Didn't you get my note?"

"Yes," he said sheepishly.

"Well ... what were your instructions?"

"The Dive Shop, July 4th ... Be there."

"The Dive Shop," she said. "Be there ... that's all it said, now isn't it," she said playfully. "Do you remember that?"

Andrew heard the inflection of her voice change, playful ... fun ... and his smile returned even though his face stayed flushed.

"Yes, 'be' at The Dive Shop, July 4th," he said holding the parchment notepaper that he had pinned to the old Polaroid photo of her.

"Good, so you understand what it means to 'be there'. And 'July 4th '; you do realize that July 4th is not like for four more days?"

"Yes, I understand," he said. He could just see her long brown hair parted down the middle, probably pulled back in a long ponytail, perfect skin, swimsuit ready body, probably still in scrubs even though working in a tent somewhere in the jungle. Somewhere in the very same jungle he had had just left for the coast.

"I always knew you were bright; it was the naval Academy wasn't it?" she teased.

"Yes, you know it was," he replied.

"What is it like?" she asked him.

"Boring without you," he replied.

"No silly, the room, I mean."

"Well, the room is kind of simple, he said. King sized bed, a lamp, writing table, and a view. But what a view," he said enjoying the ocean, the blue clear water and the white sanded beach. "It's beautiful ... just beautiful," he said. "Just like you," he added smiling into the phone.

"Oh agent Galloway, you are in too much trouble to get out of jail by showering me with sweetness. You are going to have to earn your way back into my good graces," she said laughing quietly.

"No problem. I'll work on it. Come meet me ... today. Can you get away early? Come meet me early?"

"Now that sounds a bit desperate ... do you miss me?" She egged him on a bit enjoying his wallow.

"Not desperate, but I've been thinking about you, and I'm excited to see you, that's all."

"Oh, you've been thinking about me?" She asked with a coy inflection: playful, but sincere wanting him to be thinking about her, feeling like he did.

"I've been thinking about you every day for the last seven years," he said looking down at the note pinned to a Polaroid.

"Yeah, you told me that once before," she said. "But I don't know if I believe you. I want proof. I want unequivocal proof that you have been thinking about me everyday for seven years," she giggled playfully.

"You do? Well it just so happens that I have proof right here!"

"Oh you do, do you? Well you know I'm a tough sell. I'm not just some girl you can pick up at a bar," she laughed.

Andrew lifted the note pinned to the Polaroid and

touched the well-worn edges of the homemade scotch taped laminate.

"If you get away early, I'll show the proof," he said.

"Oh, Andrew, once again your timing is bad," the nurse replied, back inside her medical tent looking down at a man in his mid thirties, lying knees to chest doubled over on a cot in the make shift medical tent that said 'Caring Hearts Medical Relief'.

"Believe it or not, I think one of our own crew in the medical group I'm traveling with has appendicitis. I can't leave him here."

"Oh, you're kidding me."

"Afraid not. A few of the guys from our medical group caught a bus heading down toward the city. I am waiting for them to bring back transportation help so we can get to the hospital in the city, but I think we may have caught a break. Some type of military group is here. I think our director has gotten them to agree to transport us down there."

"Military group? What kind of military group?" Andrew asked alarm stepping in.

"They look like a cross between police and soldiers," she said.

"OK look, stay put. I'm on my way," Andrew replied.

"Oh, how sweet, are you thinking of foraging through the jungle to come find me?"

"This is serious," he said. "I've been in this part of Central America for six months now, and this part of the world is not like what you are used to. The rules are different. Girls like you can get in trouble pretty quickly."

"Girls like me? Oh Andrew Galloway, don't you think I can take care of myself? Do you think I'm like that little puppy that needed saving?" she chided.

"It was a cat," he said, head in hands, knowing she didn't understand the grounds for his concern.

"Dog, cat, it doesn't matter. Just stay put Andrew. Don't try to come up here; you'll never find me without a guide."

"I don't need a guide. I've flown over those hills and villages at least a hundred times during STATESIDE training. I can find you."

"Andrew, sit tight. Enjoy the beach. I'll meet you at the The Dive Shop as soon as I can. Just stick to the plan," Andrew's nurse replied.

"OK," Andrew replied in an unconvincing monotone.

"Andrew, say it back to me so I know you understand. After all, I sometimes wonder about your listening skills," she said taking them both back to the time when they first met.

"I'm hearing you." Andrew smiled into the mobile phone, still holding a Polaroid picture of her along with a note. "The Dive Shop; July 4th ... Be there."

"Great! It's a date then. I'll see you at most in a few days," he heard her say.

"July 4th; it's a date," Andrew replied. "But leave your phone on," he said.

"You're sweet," he heard her say, almost feeling her smile through the phone.

"OK, got to go..."

"Wait ... don't hang up," he said into static, certain he heard the sound of an automatic weapon.

CHAPTER 18

July 4

Steward Township Hospital

0730

In the family room outside the ICU, Dr. Jon Mackenzie found Scott Galloway alone, staring out the window looking down the Valley at the beautiful white arches of the new bridge that spanned the river at the foot of Thunderbird.

"I bet that saves you a lot of time getting to work," Scott said breaking the ice.

"Legend around here is, that a young man once jumped that river, right where that bridge is, as a matter of fact, to save a cat."

"Andrew ..." his father laughed. "Sounds just like him."

"Thanks for what you did for my daughter, Scott," Dr. Mackenzie said to the commander with an outstretched hand. "I owe you one."

"Thanks, but it seems I am just trying to catch up. First me; now my son .... Funny how our lives seem to cross in extremes," Scott Galloway said to his acquaintance from long ago, referring to the first time their paths crossed during active assignment.

"I still can't believe that you were able to find me; and my platoon – off grid, off radar."

"Something in the wind, that day, Scott," Dr. Mackenzie replied with a vague smile recalling the intuitive hit that led him across the cold waters of the outer banks to find a stranded SEALs team that cold January day.

"Spider sense?" Commander Galloway laughed.

"Is that how you found me? All those years ago?"

"I really cannot explain it, Scott. Something drew me to you; intuition maybe, I don't know. The same way you know when someone is standing behind you; or when you get the unexplainable idea to call someone you haven't heard from for a while who picks up the phone and says, 'I was just thinking of you, and then you called.' It was as if you were broadcasting a radio signal with a frequency that I just happened to be tuned into."

"Sounds like ESP."

"I'm not sure about ESP, Scott."

"Are you a student of Carl Jung's work? On the collective unconsciousness?"

"In medical school briefly. But even today, ESP, intuition, and the collective unconsciousness are dismissed by science. There is no rational or medical explanation for it. It is not comprehensible by studying the brain, as it seems to exist beyond logic, beyond reason, in a different paradigm, a different dimension."

"Sounds to me like you believe in something though: something spiritual, Jon?"

"Perhaps spiritual yes. In my work; in my life, a simple principle guides me."

"Oh yeah, what is that?"

"I believe that every kindness counts, Scott. When we set our intention to help, to be of service, we make way for the miraculous to unfold. I know I can't explain it, and I know it makes no logical sense, but I believe it."

"Do you teach that to the residents?"

"I don't know that I teach them anything ... but I do try to make them aware of the power in kindness. I hope it becomes the way at this institution."

"Well I hope it works in Andrew's favor, Jon," Commander Scott Galloway said to Dr. Jon Mackenzie in a heartfelt moment of pain. "I think we would all welcome a miracle."

"I understand, Scott. And I know this looks scary, but he looks like he's doing fine. I don't think we need a miracle here. He is going to wake up and let's see if we can't get him back to you."

"Thanks Jon. My wife and I appreciate everything you are doing. Oh yeah, can you please call off the dogs … My wife got a visit from the organ harvesting team floating around here. It is making my wife extremely nervous."

"Will do, Scott. Sometimes our newer residents become overzealous in their approach to 'the case', and lose sight of 'the people'. In reasonable medical probability he will be waking up soon."

"Thanks Jon; thanks for everything."

"No problem, 'CG' "

" 'CG', " Commander Galloway smiled.

"Yes, Isn't that what your crew calls you?"

"Yes," Andrew's father smiled. "It would seem so."

CHAPTER 19

June 30, 2012

STATESIDE Training Camp
Mountains, Central America

Noon

STATESIDE Specialist Sean 'Sully' Sullivan finished collapsing his bunk and threw a packed green duffle bag down where the cot used to be. In dark green fatigues, and light green tee shirt, Sully stared across the sun-bleached shadow where Andrew Galloway's cot used to be, reveling in the feeling of freedom that had finally arrived. 'Sanctioned abdication of accountability,' he laughed recalling the words that his friend and fellow agent Andrew Galloway had spoken before packing his STATESIDE duffle bag and taking his leave from the mountain training facility down to the resort city along the coast two days ago.

23 years old, with the blond stubble on his face and a shock of hair growing out from its crew cut origins,

Sully sat up in his cot and began playing the instructions Drew left had left for him yesterday before Andrew boarded a chicken bus to the City, off to meet up with the voice he had been talking to whenever cell service allowed. "She's a nurse," Andrew had told Sully; "and she's bringing along some friends." Andrew had told him.

"Now what kind of wingman would I be if I didn't go meet him," Sully told Trent, the only other specialist left in camp, while pondering the invite to come join them after camp was broken down.

Fit and strong, Sully easily collapsed down the tent, smiling. The feeling of freedom was a good one, especially after six months of hard training. Sully couldn't help but recognize the thrilling anticipation of promise. A cold beer in the vacation sun; a few beauty queens barely covered by string and a few patches, and one week without a chain of command to follow. Sully was glad to be breaking the training camp, happy to put down the responsibility that came with medical tech support, air evacuation and field rescue. Sully, Trent and Andrew had become good friends after the time spent together finishing out the ICU suite in the big C-17 Transport Airplane that STATESIDE was to put in service back in Texas, and had gone through basic CPR and Advanced Trauma Life support. Sully had started IV lines on each of his associate agents until they had no veins left. They got checked out on STATESIDE's Apache helicopter, the Huey, and Sully had made and unmade parachutes until he could do it in his sleep. He made several jumps with Trent and Drew, had been on recon, air support, and radio and even took a helo up in the air as part of emergency pilot training. They swam open water, rode open ground and for the last six months they slept in a tent nestled up in the mountains not far from one of the nicest diving reefs in the world. 'A long week at the beach would do us all some good', Sully thought, heading into the holiday weekend. Sully pictured himself with his friends, emerging from the water, surrounded by white sand and a few sexy beach bodies with cinnamon tans. Sully chuckled, "Babes in bikini's ... nothing like it."

On his way to HQ to check out, Sully stopped by to collect Trent, but Trent's dirt bike was gone. Sully searched over to the big C-17, but no sign of Trent among the other technicians who were busily loading up the big C-17 transport cargo plane, complete with the brand spanking new 11 ICU beds.

'Trent must be at HQ checking out', Sully thought. Instead of kick starting his dirt bike to life, Sully threw his pack over the saddle, rolled the motor bike toward what was left of the camp HQ, and enjoyed the feeling of not being late.

"I like what you've done with the place, Radcoms," Sully said to the clerk. Radcoms – short for 'Radio/ communications support' was still in STATESIDE dress cammos and in the middle of packing up supplies to be loaded onto the big C-17 transport plane.

"What! Aren't you supposed to be on a dive by now?" Radcoms asked pushing up a pair of glasses that sat low on his nose, looking up at the taller agent as he came forward into the tent.

"No, D is the only one who managed to get out early," Sully said about Andrew. "Rendezvous with a lady…. Trent and I are heading out today. Have you seen him by the way? He's not in his tent and his dirt bike is gone."

"Well apparently, Trent is out searching for a chicken bus or something. Drew called Trent this morning; he needed a surveillance favor."

"Drew … he should be on the beach by now. He left yesterday."

"Yeah, going after a girl for a change huh? And I hear you two are planning on catching his fall out," Radcoms jabbed, having seen first hand how the girls seemed to collect around the athletic physique and green eyes of the usually disinterested agent.

"Yep, she's supposed to be traveling with a few friends, 'on a mission,'" Sully winked. "Not too late to change your mind. Chicken bus runs every hour!"

"Yeah right. Good luck with that ground transport. So got any intel on D's little missionary? Do we know anything about her?"

"You know Drew ... wouldn't say much; but he said she's a bolt of lightening that managed to strike him twice. I think he's carried a torch for her for a long time. Have you seen that ratty old Polaroid that he's been carrying around since Christmas."

"No, not really, but then again I'm not inclined to go through other agents things, now Sully. What's up with that?"

"Skip it."

"So, any word from your bunkmate, Radcoms? Did Trent say what time he'd be back," Sully asked the clerk. "We are supposed to catch the 1300 chicken bus tour through Central America."

"Well, I'm sorry to say, the plot has thickened. Trent is still out, and Captain Spence and Petey are meeting with the Commander about it right now. I think they are trying to put together a run. CG just told me to get COMS set up; set up after I just got it broken down and stowed, you know!"

"What are you talking about Radcoms?"

"Not that I'm advocating eaves dropping or anything ... but ..." Radcoms thumbed a nod behind the dark green tarp. Sully, listening from behind the tarp, could hear the voices of Captain Christopher Spence, the pilot, Lieutenant Rob Pete and The STATESIDE Commander, 'CG' as the men called him.

————

STATESIDE Field HQ Tent
Captain Chris Spence
Lieutenant Rob Pete
Commander Scott Galloway

"With the goddamn Peace Corps?" Sully heard Captain Spence rail in restrained laughter from behind the anything but soundproof closed tarp. Sully pictured Captain Spence leaning hips back against the desk, strong, sun reddened and peeling forearms folded, his Nordic skin tones not taking sun well. "You have got to be kidding me CG!" Captain Spence said to the Commander.

Sully stayed his distance, listening to Captain Spence and the Commander without being seen.

"Not the Peace Corps, Chris," Sully heard the Commander say back to Captain Christopher Spence.

"How did you get roped into this one CG?" Sully heard Captain Spence ask the commander.

"Trent called it in before we lost COMS … Andrew called Trent."

"Andrew? What is he doing calling anyone? Isn't he off on R and R?"

"He is down at the coast, in the City; supposed to meet up with a hospital group on a medical mission trip not far from here. According to Trent, the group found some trouble and needs some medical assist along with a lift out."

"What kind of assist?"

"Well, something about a chicken bus accident. Trent thinks two are banged up a bit but are ambulatory and can still travel. But apparently one of the nurses is still in the village in a hut; with a patient; belly pain … possible appendicitis."

"And how do we know all this marvelous intel?"

"Trent is out in the field with eyes on the bus; and Andrew's friend is in a makeshift medical hut in the village where they were working. They are supposed to be close by … just a few clicks from here."

"OK CG, spill it … what's really up?"

"The medical group is out of Steward Township Hospital, in Meza."

"Steward Township, CG; the hospital near Fort Clemmons; in Meza? Are you still trying to lock down that contract with them?"

"Yes, I am, it would be nice to partner with Steward Township Hospital now that we have the contract with Fort Clemmons."

"Yes, that landing strip will come in handy for the big C- 17," Captain Spence acknowledged.

"Looks like Steward Township Hospital has everything we need," the Commander added; "they are a level one trauma center and can handle complex evacs."

"So, one good turn deserves another?"

"I get you Spence," the Commander replied. "I am not doing this to get the contract with Steward Township. It would be nice if that happens, but my intention is not to coerce them into anything."

"You have to admit, nice goddamn piece of luck though, right CG? Oh but wait a minute – you are the guy who doesn't believe in luck, right? The guy who always says that nothing happens by chance; and there is no such thing as an accident."

"That's right Spence. I've seen it too many times; accidents are the unexpected … the unanticipated," Commander said.

"A Glitch in the Matrix CG?"

The Commander laughed and raised his eyebrows looking at Spence.

"I've heard young Andrew proclaim that a time or two."

"You've got to admit Chris," the Commander said to Captain Spence, "I think we have all seen Providence intercede at times."

"The divine breaking into the affairs of men? Sounds like mythology if you ask me."

"Yes, yes … Chris," CG laughed with Captain Spence. "I can see that side of it too!"

"Well … I live in the real world CG; where failing to plan is planning to fail. So what's the plan, Commander?" Captain Spence asked.

"You look flight ready, CG," Petey said, as the pilot eyed the Commander who was wearing high top boots and cammos. At fifty, the Commander, with a hint of grey sprinkled through his light brown hair, filled out his flight suit well. Committed to exercise, time in the weight room was shared with the track and the pool.

"Well here's a plan CG," Captain Spence interjected playfully. "Let's pick up the chicken bus fallout, along with young Andrew's little honey, and her casualty victim and fly them all home in a state of the art air transport hospital. Then we can knock on Steward's door and say 'Surprise!'"

"Something like that," the Commander said with a smile. "It wouldn't hurt to make a good impression on the folks at Steward by making an impressive entrance. We can salvage that Caring Hearts Mission trip, and bring them safely home, and make a grand impression on the Steward Folks in one fell swoop."

"And get a nice long contract to boot, huh CG?"

"With any luck," the Commander winked. "That would be nice if it happens."

"OK CG, so what is the plan?"

"Well, I'm going to hop down there and pick up the nurse and the belly pain, then check out what kind of trouble Trent found in the field. I'll bring them all back here in time for wheels up."

"Who's flying with you CG?"

"Well, Sully is the only other agent left in camp, but he is either with Andrew or probably already half way to the coast for R and R."

"No I'm not," Sully said, smiling, folding back the forest green opening to the tent and walking in with Radcoms following closely behind. "What's up?"

"Well," Captain Spence jumped in, "Andrew called Trent who called CG, here, and asked him to pick up his date that is travelling with some Peace Corp medical missionary volunteer group. It seems they found some trouble while rebuilding a village about 5 clicks south of here. Apparently there is a bus ... a chicken bus, if I understand right, involved ... chicken bus must have a flat tire down in the valley because as long as Trent has been out there he's got to be jacking up the spare."

"Nice Spence," the commander scowled.

"Well that's just about the truth, isn't it CG?"

"First off, they are not with the Peace Corps," CG explained to specialists Sully and Radcoms. "Andrew called Trent about some trouble involving a group out of Steward Township Hospital in Meza, Texas volunteering on a medical mission trip – you know improving living quarters, education and medicine for locals."

"Oh wow, Steward Township Hospital, in Meza Texas. You've been after them for a while now, huh CG?"

"That's right Sully. I've been after them for a while," CG responded all the while eyeing Captain Spence.

"I didn't say a thing!" Captain Spence said feigning innocence with both hands up.

"And while details are sketchy, one passenger is too sick to travel. We think a few others are injured not far from here … something about a bus mishap on the ground. I offered to give them a lift home … that's all."

"Makes sense…. We are going that way anyway … but why is Trent spotting the chicken bus?" Sully asked.

"Because Greyhound stopped providing nonstop runs down here," Spence said deadpan.

"I see … pay it forward, huh CG?"

"Jeez Sully, not you, too!" Spence laughed.

"I guess I've been hanging around the Commander and Drew too long. Speaking of the missing, does Drew know about the plan yet?"

"Apparently young Andrew forgot to charge his cell

phone, and let's just say … well COMS is still a problem," Captain Spence interjected. "I have been informed by the radio/communication specialist, that we, here at STATESIDE's luxurious mountain resort, well Radcoms, is it fair to say no receivers are yet functional?"

"I'm on it Captain, but just so you know, my orders were to take down the uplink from STATESIDE central, and all the mobile uplinks are already stowed," Radcoms offered. "It isn't my fault. I didn't know about this until just a few minutes ago."

"So are you going to fly CG?" Sully asked the Commander.

"Yes, Sully, I'll hop down there in the Huey, in STS-1; I should be able to pick up the group and transport them back here in the Huey ready to move out on schedule … wheels up by 1600, as planned," said the commander. "Boy, I sure could use a few volunteers to hop down there with me," CG scanned the room. "Seems like most of the team is off service."

"I'll fly with you CG," offered Petey. The 25-year-old black-eyed pilot was staring at a computer screen, smiling while scratching the perpetual black facial stubble that seemed to grow minutes after his morning shave.

"Oh yeah?" asked Spence. "What gives? You are willing to give up some leave time, are you?"

"Awe, you know, Cappy …" Lieutenant Pete said to

Captain Spence, "CG's trying to help out the company and all, and the value of paying it forward ..." Petey smiled up at Sully.

"They're hot aren't they?" Sully asked the pilot. "The nurses ... right?"

Sully caught a glimpse of a social media page that was still up on the laptop before Petey slapped the cover closed.

"Hey, let me see that...."

"Sorry, coms is out, can't get it back friend," Petey said with a twinkle in his dark eyes, as he flipped his wavy dark black hair off to the side.

"OK," Sully looked up, "I'm in too!" Sully said looking around the tent. "Besides, I won't leave without Trent anyway. Don't leave your wingman, right CG!"

"That's right, Sully," CG smiled.

"Petey can copilot and I will ride Med-Tech support ... in case there are any bruises or scrapes that need tending to ..." Sully said with a mischievous grin.

"Thanks, Sully, I owe you both," the commander laughed, looking at Petey and Sully.

"You two go get your gear. We'll hop over in STS 1 and start aerial recon," the Commander informed the men. "Trent on a dirt bike, and a disabled chicken bus on the only road between here and the coast should be easy enough to spot from the air," the commander said.

Spence watched the two agents walk out of the green

mesh tent, and said to the commander, "Look CG, you've got more important things to do than fly down there yourself. Why don't you finish packing up base camp and load the transport. I'll hop down there with Petey and Sully on STS 1 and get them back here," said Spence.

"Thanks Chris," said the commander to Captain Spence extending his hand. "I owe you one as well."

"What a piece of luck huh CG; we just secured that landing strip at Fort Clemmons, in Meza, and now we get to knock on the door of Steward?"

"Yes …" the Commander said, relenting. "Nice piece of luck. And it would be nice to have a medical affiliate with a friendly rooftop. It would be nice to have Steward Township Hospital in our pocket with the C-17 basing out of Fort Clemmons."

"So who is your contact at Steward?"

"Dr. Jon Mackenzie. Ex-military. We crossed paths a long time ago. I owe him my life actually; but he was the one who made the introductions to get the ball rolling."

"So let me guess … it just so happens that this nurse is the General's daughter, isn't she?" Spence asked.

"He's a colonel …" CG smiled.

———

1400

Still in cammos, Sully did a quick inventory of his medic bag. What does one really need for a chicken bus rescue, he thought. He ran down the ABC's with one oral airway, one ET tube, size seven. Can't imagine having to use this, he thought, as he had never had to place an Endotracheal Tube in the field before, even in a high acuity setting.

The appy could probably use some IV fluids … better take this, Sully thought grabbing a few bags of normal saline and lactated ringers solution. That ought to do it, Sully finished, satisfied with an ambu bag, 25 gauge needles, syringes, IV fluid, three rolls of tape, gauze, and antibiotic cream. Sully zipped his bag closed and threw it over his shoulder as he left.

Sully, the last to arrive, jumped up into the Huey and strapped in daydreaming as they lifted over the hills and headed southeast to the water.

"Hey Petey," Sully shouted up to the pilot, "just tell it to me straight … the group of nurses … they were hot, weren't they."

———

Airborne over the jungle
Central America
15:01 PM

The STATESIDE Huey hovered over what looked like an old yellow school bus stalled on a dirt road in the valley of the Central American Mountains, when an explosion ripped through the valley from the river just ahead.

"Over there, Petey take us in," said Captain Spence to the pilot. Petey brought the helo in for a closer look and Captain Spence pulled out a pair of binoculars as did med tech specialist Sully, and they scanned the horizon over the bridgeless river below, hovering over what was left of the recipient of the artillery strike.

Specialist Sullivan, wearing his green med tech bag embossed with the STATESIDE logo over his shoulder like a satchel, heard the sound of a small engine that strained against an open throttle as it rattled through the valley from the top of the hill.

"Over there Cappy," Sully said to Captain Spence, as both sets of binoculars found the scooter as it appeared on the far side of the river. Med Tech Sullivan and Captain Spence watched the rider race the scooter down the slope of the mountainous thicket to a makeshift riverbank launch point. With the bridge gone, the rider took the small scooter airborne, flying high up over the river twenty feet in the air. Sully saw the rider lose control of the scooter mid jump, flying upside down half way over the river. Sully watched the rider somehow salvage the position by completing a summersault, taking the scooter around in midair. The rider landed the scooter rear wheel down like Evil Kneivel, before bouncing as the front wheel hit. As the rider regained control of the bike, the ground exploded just behind the scooter; Sully and Spence watched the rider fly forward, ejected head first over the handle bars on the near side of the river. The rider was facedown with his head toward the scooter and was not moving.

"Take us down, Petey," Captain Spence said to the pilot as he pointed to the near side of the river where the rider was down. Petey found a suitable landing zone in a clearing near the position of the toppled scooter, and positioned the Huey for descent.

One hundred yards from touchdown the crew of the Huey heard the sound of a launched missile. They felt STS 1 rock violently and heard the sound of metal tearing away from the hull of the helicopter as the Huey rocked sideways.

"The sled is gone Cappy," Sully reported up to captain, both watching the landing sled tear loose from STS 1.

"Can you get us down?" Captain Spence asked Petey as the pilot maneuvered the helo to center.

"I'll try, but we're going to bounce," Petey shouted into his headset, as the pilot positioned the Huey to land in a clearing near the river's edge.

Moments later, the STATESIDE team of three jumped out and took cover behind their lopsided, grounded helicopter.

"The rocket came from the far side of the river," Captain Spence said peering through the open cargo bay.

"They must have taken out the bridge after they crossed the river," Petey noted.

"How bad, Petey?" Captain Spence asked the pilot. Petey stayed low and out of sight of any militia; he ran the perimeter and inspected the damage to the helicopter. He pushed back, gaining perspective, quietly studying the listing pitch of the hull. Petey tilted his head like a golfer studying a put, matching the pitch of the Huey and it's missing landing sled, as the curved blade stood intact, piercing the surface of the ground.

"Well, sir," said, Petey said as he huddled back with Captain Spence and Medical Specialist Sully along side of the injured Huey, "we lost the landing sled and the blade is grounded, but she looks like she'll fly. Sitting her down again may be a problem...."

Captain Spence put a pair of military binoculars back up to his eyes again and scanned the horizon and found the downed rider. After a few seconds he said, "Come on, get up, get up," as if the unknown rider downed over a thousand yards away could hear him. But the body just beyond the scooter was not moving.

"God damn it!" Captain Spence spit out. "Petey get that blade free ... Sully, let's go get him."

———

1507

Sully hit the ground first dropping his green canvas

medical bag and shouted to Captain Spence. "Cappy, it's Andrew!"

"Andrew?" Captain Spence exclaimed. "What the ... I thought he was supposed to be at the coast!"

"I don't know Cappy," Sully said to Spence; "but he's in trouble."

"Come on Sully, let's get him over to the Huey," Captain Spence said stepping over the scooter. "I got him Cappy," Sully said to Spence, and Sully threw Andrew over his shoulder and began running back to the helo.

————

1510

Spence and Sully scrambled back over to the Huey with Andrew in and out of consciousness. They stepped past the landing sled no longer attached to the base of the helicopter and approached the pilot. Captain Spence ducked under the wilting pitch of the blades above them.

"What's the story with the cowboy?" Petey asked pointing to the victim as Sully slung the injured body on the ground in front of the cabin door.

"You are not going to believe this Petey," Captain Spence shouted to the pilot, "he's ours ... now let's get those blades moving."

"Andrew?" Petey said, shaking his head. "No...."

"Get us straight, get those blades free," Captain Spence instructed the pilot.

Petey gave the Huey one more shove tilting the lopsided helicopter far enough on point to free the grounded blade of the helicopter, then jumped into the cockpit.

Sully kneeled astride Andrew preparing to load him in the cargo bay of the Huey. "Cappy," Sully said to Captain Spence, eyes glued to the puffy face of the rescue as he lay at the foot of the Huey, "he's swelling badly."

Spence watched Sully sit on top of Andrew's body like he imagined an older brother would pin his prey in a wrestling match. "You OK Sully?"

"D man, stay with me," Sully said to Andrew as the bruised body lost awareness. "You are going to be OK."

———

1508

"Petey ... where you at?" asked Spence of the pilot.

"She'll lift," Petey said as he watched the wobble.

"OK, we are a go in sixty seconds," Spence alerted his team.

"Sixty seconds?" Petey shouted up from the cockpit of the Huey in a panic. "Sir, we don't have sixty seconds! Cappy, if we don't lift out now we're gonna get lit!!"

Spence looked up at Petey who was pointing out of the window of the Huey to the field, where a camouflaged militia soldier appeared from behind a dilap-idated school bus. He was loading a hand held rocket launcher aimed directly at their broadside.

"God damn it!" shouted Spence.

"Petey, crank it! Lift on my go! Sully, strap him down back there, and don't lose that goddamn airway!"

"Five," Captain Spence checked the path of the blade spinning well with the Huey now under full power.

"Four," Captain Spence checked on Petey in the cab-in working the helo.

"Three," Captain Spence checked on Sully sitting on top of the downed agent.

"Two," Captain Spence saw the rocket launcher aimed to kill.

"One," Captain Spence shouted, "Go! GO!! GOO!"

Chapter 20

July 40

Steward Township Hospital
Family Room

0800

"And 'CG' would like to thank you on behalf of STATESIDE; thanks for making it right with the Hospital – I know that drop-in was awkward to say the least and it made a lot of people angry. I am sorry the crew couldn't release any details, still classified until this morning, you know," explained Commander Galloway.

"No problem, Scott," Dr. Mackenzie said extending his hand. "This retired Navy officer would like to thank you for evac-ing my daughter out of the jungles of central America to Houston."

"You should be proud, Jon. She seems like a lovely girl."

Steward Township Hospital
Staff Lounge

08:30

"So, it turns out," Ginny finished debriefing Dr. Williams in the staff lounge, "that Beth was rescued by Andrew's father who had piloted the STATESIDE helicopter that swooped in and pulled her out. So here is our Bethie involved with this Andrew, rescued by Andrew's father, just as he was trying to rescue her!"

———

July 4

Steward Township Hospital
ICU bed-1

09:00 AM

"Amanda, this is Dr. Jon Mackenzie," Commander Scott Galloway introduced. "His team is taking care of Andrew. He is also helping us with the STATESIDE medical project here at Steward Township."

"Nice to meet you, Dr. Mackenzie. My husband speaks very highly of you. It seems that I owe you for the lives of the two most important men in my family."

"An honor. And I have you both to thank for the safe return of my daughter, Beth. Andrew's valor is admirable; I am sure I have you both to thank for that."

"Good morning Sister Mary Grace," Dr. Mackenzie said to Sister Mary Grace as she sat with his daughter at Andrew's bedside chair. "We could sure use a bit of good luck on this one," Dr. Mackenzie winked to his daughter next to the Sister. And with that simple glance, Beth began crying....

"Are you OK sweetie?" her father asked.

"Oh dad, its all my fault! If I hadn't gone down there, if I had not been there, none of this would have ever happened."

"You can't think like that Beth ... things happen badly sometimes because they do. We see it every day here. Doesn't make sense to us, but we cannot always see the complete picture. Look at the other side of the equation. What if you weren't there? They all might be dead now. You stayed and helped, and that's what counts. That young man you nursed had a bad case of appendicitis, and you helped him though it. You did good, sweetie. I couldn't be more proud of you."

"No dad, he's the real hero. He risked his life for me."

Sister Mary Grace smiled as she listened to the love between father and daughter express in action. She looked at the patient in the bed, and silently breathed the word 'Valor'. Life risked for the sake of life, she reflected. It is said to be one of the last lessons in the progression.

"He's going to be all right, dad, isn't he?" Beth paused and composed herself a bit. "Come on Andrew ... wake up ... wake up or you will be late for our date ....."

CHAPTER 21

July 4th

Steward Township Hospital
ICU-1
Meza Texas

14:00

In confusion inside the body of ICU-1, Andrew felt as if the tube was choking the very life from him....

'I can't breath ... got to get rid of this', he thought and he bit down hard on the tube lodged deeply in his throat. 'Got to get free,' he thought.

Andrew struggled fiercely, in the dark, summoning air up from his lungs and exhaling forcefully, like blowing trapped, stagnant air from within oxygen deprived lungs at the end of a race.

"Code Blue, ICU-1"
"Code Blue ICU-1"

Williams was the first to arrive, silencing his code pager as he ran into the room. The still body lie lifelessly quiet, the blue ET tube tossed over the bed, the bed covers tossed to the side, as if an epic battle was waged.

"He extubated himself! Get an airway."

Ginny slapped a mask over the patient's mouth, and began forcing air into a stem-like tube. "Airway clear," she said.

"Begin chest compressions," Williams barked out!

"One, two, three, breathe ... one, two, three breathe...."

Amanda Galloway looked on in horror. It was as if her worst fear was materializing right in front of her eyes.

"Andrew," she whimpered "hold on son ... you can make it."

"Check for a pulse!"

"No pulse, resume CPR."

"Charge the paddles!"

"Pads set: ready to cardiovert!"

"120 joules, set; all clear!"

Amanda watched her son lift off the bed, six inches in the air as the electric wave surged through his body, the smell of flesh burning taking her by surprise.

"Check for a pulse!" She heard.

"No pulse; 240 joules; center that pad!" She watched the medical team hover over her son.

"Pad in place; clear!" She heard as electrified paddles were placed over her son's chest again.

Amanda watched 240 joules of energy lift Andrew's body off the table.

'Stop,' she thought to herself. 'Stop it.'

"360: clear!"

When Andrew landed on the floor after a second and third shock of 360 joules, Amanda Galloway stood back, hoping, but knowing. Knowing in her heart that she had lost him. She had lost her only son.

"Still nothing!"

"OK, we need to tube him.... Begin CPR ... who is marking time?"

"Begin CPR...."

Amanda saw the medical team approach and drop down on the floor and put their hands on her son's chest, and blow air into his mouth.

"Stop!" She said out loud in a commanding voice. "Stop!"

The waveform of sound brought all action to a resounding stop.

"That is enough ... he has been through enough ... let him be ..." she said to the stunned medical team standing sheepishly over her son.

Williams and Ginny moved back from their posts near the head of the bed of the lifeless body.

Dr. Mackenzie emerged quickly, with Scott Galloway followed by Beth who dropped to the ground on her knees in front of Sister Mary Grace who sat in the bedside chair.

———

"He is gone, Scott … he is gone. Our son is gone."

CHAPTER 22

TV 14406 felt a jolt of electricity and he was aware of paddles on his chest. Andrew felt his body convulse from the current and Andrew felt his heart beating, fast at first, and then he felt it slow down. In that moment, his mind quieted and Andrew wondered what death would be like. As he waited to die, he felt air expire through his nose and mouth and he felt his chest heave. He wondered what his last breath would feel like. He wondered if his last breath would feel like the last breath of an all out swim as he stretched for the wall draining his lung capacity forcing out the used breath of life. With eyes closed, preparing to surrender life, Andrew listened to the sound of his own his heartbeat. Beat ... Beat ... Beat ... Beat ... until it stopped. In the silence Andrew stepped up and out of his body like pushing himself over the ledge of the pool after a workout. He stepped into the warmth of a radiant light he had never before experienced. Unsure if it was a moment or an hour within the radiant light he heard a sound … tick … tick … tick … as if his heart began beating anew. The measured beats, he realized, was the sound of time passing in seconds. The source of the sound, he realized was coming from the radiant light. And then as if coming into frame from an out of focus camera lens, Andrew saw the familiar countenance of a bespectacled figure with grey hair and black horn rimmed glasses, staring at the face of a hand-held stopwatch that was attached to his neck by a black-corded rope.

"Mr. Sebastian?" Andrew asked, studying the face and shape of his coach and mentor.

"Is that you?"

"Yes, it is I," Mr. Sebastian said, depressing the button on the stopwatch hanging around his neck. "It's good to be with you again, Andrew."

"Mr. Sebastian! How can this be, I thought you were … are… "

"Congratulations, Andrew!" Mr. Sebastian said excitedly, "You have reached an exit."

"An exit?"

"Yes. You can go on if you'd like," Mr. Sebastian said

pointing to a closed door, brimming with light, as if the top, bottom and sides were glowing with a light that could not be contained.

Andrew opened the door and experienced the light. His mind grew silent and all thought stopped as an infinite Presence was made manifest. Within the light of the Presence, he experienced a state that he had never known before. He felt calm, and warm and loved and he experienced an illuminated state beyond all time, beyond all description. The feeling intensified and he felt as if his very essence was vibrating with the energy of the Presence. The energy, he knew as if by revelation, was love.

In the room of light and love, Andrew felt the power of an infinite love and a state of peacefulness followed. He understood that love was the nature of his essence; and just like the Presence, it had no beginning and no end, just as he had no beginning and no end. Life goes to life, never-ending. In the light of awareness Andrew felt joy, and Andrew realized peace.

Andrew stepped as if back, back into the ether where he once again experienced his former coach and friend.

"Mr. Sebastian. It is amazing."

"Yes, Andrew, congratulations."

"But what are you doing here Mr. Sebastian?"

"I've got one more soul contract to fulfill, Andrew before I go on."

"Soul contract? What do you mean by that, Mr. Sebastian?"

"Each of us is born into the matrix of life and time with certain agreements, contracts if you will. We each have opportunity to complete certain tasks and take on particular challenges in each of our lifetimes. The completion of those tasks and challenges help us repay debts, and accumulate grace. Often times our destiny pulls us forward where we meet tasks and challenges that serve our soul. Soul work is something quite extraordinary Andrew. You would be surprised by the mighty forces that become engaged in the synchronicity of such soul work."

"Synchronicity; what do you mean by that?"

"I mean the orchestration of it all, Andrew. Nothing happens by chance; and there are no co-incidences. What seems like a co-incidence is not. What seems like an accident is not. All of the events and people in your life – even the smallest chance encounters – have provided opportunity for the work of your soul Andrew. The Matrix of life in time has been and continues to be opportunity, Andrew: opportunity through choice and will, Andrew. Life in time offers opportunity to pay back debts, to gain grace, to transcend and ascend in your understanding and awareness. It is a remarkable opportunity to be born human, Andrew."

"But I thought we finished all of our business before I left for California. Before ... you died...."

"Things are not always as they seem, and things appear to be what they are not Andrew."

"I am not sure what you mean, Mr. Sebastian."

"Perhaps a lesson for another lifetime, Andrew. Go on, Andrew. Peace awaits."

CHAPTER 23

July 4, 2012

Steward Township Hospital
ICU-bed-1

1:44 PM

After the body of Andrew Galloway hit the floor and after the last breath of the boy known as TV 14406 had been taken, Sister Mary Grace reverently hung her head in silent prayer.

"May the Peace of the Lord be with you, now and forever," she said with love in her heart, reveling in the sanctity of the moment.

In the bedside chair, Sister Mary Grace began to sing, quietly, sweetly, in perfect pitch with angelic resonance.

"Make me a channel of your Peace ..."

As she sang, she felt her spine begin to tingle and she felt a warmth in her chest, and she felt an energy flow as if out of her heart, as if of its own accord, as if up to heaven above.

————

After the timelessness of revelation, there was a sudden awareness within Andrew's essence. He heard a voice lifted in song, as if through a megaphone ascending up and through the door back within the matrix of physical time.

Once again aware of life in time, Andrew was aware of the scene below, at the bedside, as if hovering over the body he had just let go.

Andrew recognized his mother's face, and he heard her whisper in sadness,

"Andrew I love you son."

His father's face appeared next, and he heard him say,

"I love you, son."

And then another voice pushed into his awareness,

"I love you Andrew.... I do ... Andrew ... I love you! You promised me, Andrew Galloway!" And Beth's face appeared with tears rolling down her cheeks. "You promised me we'd meet ... July 4th," Beth pleaded with tears flowing freely. "You promised," she whispered no longer able to speak.

————

Go back, Andrew willed himself. Go back.

————

A moment later, Andrew heard the ticking of a watch. Mr. Sebastian appeared before him once again from within the ether.

"They think I am dead, Mr. Sebastian," Andrew said, sensing the anguish, and the grief and intense sadness of his family below. "They have no concept of the beauty and the peace of life beyond physical life, do they Mr. Sebastian."

"No, they do not. Very few understand from within the matrix of life in time," Mr. Sebastian replied.

"What if I don't want to go on, Mr. Sebastian? What if I want to go back?" Andrew asked intensely aware of the anguish and grief of those below.

"Is there a way to go back?"

"Yes ... there is a way, Andrew. There is a channel, a channel of Peace that will carry you back into time."

———

Sister Mary Grace knew it was happening again. In the moment of death, in the moment of tragedy, she couldn't help but feel love at the thought of the beauty of it all. Ascension: glorious graduation from physical life. In her heart, she knew that this boy had done all he needed to do to go on, and that was perfect.

Sister Mary Grace lifted her voice in song, as her spine tingled and her chest tightened. Her words were barely audible now as she was nearly overcome by the tremendous explosion of energy within her chest, as if emotion was made physical flowing out into the world and up into the heavens above. She closed her eyes and folded herself over in the chair. Slumped forward she whispered, "Make me a channel of your Peace...."

———

"Through willingness and surrender, the miraculous is possible Andrew," Mr. Sebastian said. "You can go back, Andrew. She is waiting for you."

"I think I understand, Mr. Sebastian. I think I see the way back," Andrew said aware of the energy flow emanating from within the matrix of time.

Andrew surrendered to the moment. His spirit followed the flow of energy back down to its source emanating up from the heart-center of the nun at a bedside chair. In a stunning moment of spirit, the two became aware of each other.

"Thank you ..." he messaged to Sister Mary Grace of Souls. "Thank you for helping me find my way back," he said without words.

"No, thank you," her spirit messaged to him. "Thank you for helping me complete the work of my soul."

Andrew and Sister Mary Grace shared the holy moment together until the flow of loving energy emanating from the heart center of Sister Mary Grace burst open with color and light, like a sun turning supernova.

"Mr. Sebastian ... wait. If I go back she will ..."

"Nothing can happen without the soul's consent Andrew. It is what she wants, or it could not be."

"To be a channel of Peace," Andrew said.

"Yes, Andrew. To be a channel of Peace."

When the burst of light exploded forth, Andrew's essence re-integrated itself into the physical body: the power of his spirit nurturing and reactivating the body.

———

July 4, 2012
ICU bed-1
12:30

The audible sound of a heart beating was the first sign of life, and movement soon followed. In ordinary consciousness, Andrew opened his green eyes to find Beth kissing his lips, crying in sadness. When she felt the movement of eyelashes on her moist cheek, she pulled back, looked down and exclaimed,

"Andrew!"

"Do that again," he whispered with a gruff and hoarse voice, and he pulled her close to him.

"Andrew.... You are alive.... Thank God.... Welcome back!"

"It's a miracle," Ginny whispered to Williams as they saw their patient open his eyes. "He was dead, wasn't he?"

"It's a miracle all right Gin. In all my years I have never seen anything like it. I wouldn't have believed it if I hadn't seen it with my own two eyes," Williams said as he put his arm around Ginny's shoulder and pulled her close in an embrace appropriate to the moment. "Hey, I was just wondering, what do you think about Houston?"

"A miracle?" Simi asked. "Where is the miracle?"

"Life is the miracle ..." Dr. Mackenzie said, standing at the foot of Andrew's bed staring over his daughter's shoulder, glancing up at Dr. Simi.

"I don't know. He woke up! But he was supposed to wake up; after all he wasn't hurt that badly." Dr. Simi walked out of the room talking to the interns. "Well, looks like I won't be scrubbing in with the harvest team," Simi said. "I wonder if the depolarizing agents stopped his heart. I've seen that happen a few times at St. Stephen's last year. Maybe I can get a paper out of this. We need to review this one. Let's review."

Simi placed his fingers on his forehead and began to construct the abstract of the reportable events here.

"First a head injury; intubated in the field; self-extubated; then codes ... 120, 240, 360; hits the deck; stop code; wait; then wakes up.... I better check the chart; make sure I didn't miss anything."

As Dr. Simi walked toward the door to the hallway chart station, he gently brushed past the nun in the bedside chair.

"That Nun was here the whole time," Simi thought with a chuckle. "We ought to ask her if she saw any miracle."

"Sister, excuse me ... Sister Mary Grace?"

But Sister Mary Grace did not move. Sister Mary Grace of Souls, remained still in the chair, eyes closed, heart no longer beating, smiling contentedly, her spirit soaring to new heights within a celestial realm beyond a beauty that she had ever thought imaginable.

"And in Dying, we are born to eternal life ...."

The end.